MERCENARY

BLADE ASUNDER BOOK 1

PAPERBACK
FANTASY

MERCENARY

JON KILN

CHAPTER 1

Ganry and Myriam made slow progress. They didn't speak. Partly to avoid making any unnecessary noise and partly because Ganry was annoyed with himself for having got unwittingly caught up in whatever mess was unfolding in the Kingdom of Palara. Eventually the creek that they had been following crossed under a bridge, and he decided to chance their luck on the road for a while, heading in the general direction of Castle Locke.

"Do you know where you're going?" asked Myriam quietly, sitting behind Ganry on his horse.

"Not exactly, but Castle Locke lies due west from the Kingdom of Palara, so we're heading the right way." He waved his hand in a vague westerly direction. "Why is Locke a safe haven for you anyway? Who's waiting for you there?"

"My mother's family hold Castle Locke."

They rode on in silence for a while.

As they rounded a bend in the road they came upon an armed road block.

"Halt! Who goes there?" challenged one of the soldiers.

Ganry quickly assessed the situation. Two soldiers, the one who spoke with his hand on his sword hilt, and the other with an arrow held loosely in his bow. He knew that the archer would pose the biggest problem. Even if they turned to gallop away, the bowman could easily shoot their horse down.

"It's them!" The archer raised his bow.

Without hesitation Ganry pulled a knife from his boot and threw it at the archer, hitting him high in the shoulder. The arrow sailed harmlessly over their heads. He spurred his horse, Bluebell, forward, and rode directly at the remaining soldier, drawing one of his short blades. In one smooth motion he slashed at the soldier's face as Bluebell pushed past. The solider bellowed in pain and fell off his mount. His comrade, with a knife in his shoulder, was none too keen to follow them. Ganry urged Bluebell on without looking back, and they remained at a canter until they had put several miles between them.

Myriam turned around but did not see any sign of pursuit. "They're not following us. Are we safe for now?"

"Princess, we are a long way from safe," cautioned Ganry. "Those soldiers will call for reinforcements and will be after us in no time. Plus, there's no knowing what lies ahead. We have a couple more hours of daylight left, then we'll need to find somewhere to spend the night." Ganry turned Bluebell off the road and returned to the forest trails where they were less likely to encounter soldiers or other travelers. They followed the creek, pushing deeper into the forest, always heading to the west.

"So it seems that your Uncle is not that keen for you to leave the castle," observed Ganry wryly, breaking the silence. He might as well try to learn more about what the the hell was going on. "Are you ready to explain why I'm fighting Palaran soliders, with a Palaran Princess?"

Myriam didn't respond for a time. Ganry thought she might have fallen asleep. He heard her sigh softly. "My father has held the throne of Palara for the last twenty years," began Myriam. "He has one brother, my uncle, Duke Harald. Harald has never married. His focus has always been on our kingdom's army and our defenses. It's been a relatively peaceful period for our Kingdom, a time of prosperity. My father never really discusses affairs of state with me, but things seemed to begin to sour between them last summer. My uncle wanted to mount a campaign to expand our Kingdom, to over-power our weaker neighbors. My father refused."

Ganry stifled a yawn. He wasn't really interested anymore, but talking would help keep him awake. "So how did you escape the coup?"

"Leonidavus, my tutor, had become worried about the tension between my father and my uncle. For the last few weeks one of my handmaidens slept in my bed, and I slept in one of the spare rooms in Leonidavus's chambers. When my uncle took control and had my family arrested, I just had just enough time to escape

3

before they realized that the girl in my bed was not me."

Ganry was impressed with the subterfuge, and the young blond girls resilience. "And tell me again, why is your uncle hunting you?"

"He wants to kill me so I no longer have a claim to the throne. Either that or wants to marry me to cement his own claim." Ganry could hear her teeth clench. "I would slit my wrists before marrying him."

"I see," nodded Ganry. He tried to change the subject. Might as well find out a bit more about the reception they were likely to get. "So how well do you know your mother's family?"

Myriam shivered in the growing cold, and the emerging dusk. "Not very well. My grandfather, my mother's father, died when she was quite young. It is my grandmother that is the head of the house now. They control all the land in the Berghein Valley. My tutor, Leonidavus, was from Berghein. I am sure that I will find sanctuary there. My grandmother will protect me."

The creek that they were following eventually led them to an old mill with an inn next to it, set back from the road. Ganry went inside to check whether they had any rooms available. Myriam sat patiently on Bluebell, who had dropped his head to snack on the lush grass that was growing nearby. The forest was quiet. She could hear the wheel of the mill turning slowly as the water rushed through it, creaking and groaning.

"I've booked us one room," said Ganry as he emerged from the inn. "I've said that you are my daughter, traveling home to our farm in the west. Try and keep yourself hidden as much as possible, and don't talk to anyone." He led Bluebell around the back of the inn to the stables and made sure that he had food and water for the night, before he escorted Myriam upstairs to the small room that they would be sharing.

"Thank you," said Myriam softly as she sat on one of the narrow beds.

"For what?" asked Ganry, the evening light catching the tears that glistened on the cheeks of Myriam.

"For helping me. For protecting me."

"Just doing my job," nodded Ganry gruffly, embarrassed by the display of vulnerability and the fragility of the cargo that he had been entrusted with. He opened the window of their room and breathed deeply as he looked out over the forest. The air was still, the forest was quiet. *The calm before the storm*, he thought grimly.

The last ten years on the road had left Ganry feeling exhausted and emotionally drained. He had seen things that he would not have believed possible: the cruelty of men, the evil caused by greed. He too had done a lot of things that he was not proud of, things that disturbed his dreams and kept him awake at night.

Ganry laid his weapons out on his bed. He began cleaning the short blade that he had used to fight off the soldier at the road block, wiping the blood away. The throwing knife that he had used on the archer would have to be replaced. He was disappointed about that. It was one of his favorites. Light and easy to carry but deadly accurate in the hands of an experienced fighter.

His most treasured weapon was his long sword. Forged by the mysterious Grimlock blade-smiths, it was one of the last remaining swords of it's kind. No one knows what happened to the fabled Grimlocks, and their secret blacksmithing techniques died with them. Ganry picked up the sword reverently, and gently ran his finger down the length of the dark blade, admiring the craftsmanship, the strength, and the power of the one constant in his life. He sheathed the sword and pulled out another of his daggers, handing it to Myriam.

"You should have a weapon, just in case." Ganry liked this blade too, and was reluctant to give it away. He had a strange fondness for all his weapons. They were his only family now. He briefly considered her earlier threat, and wondered if this would be the blade she would use to slit her wrists, if Harald ever forced their marriage.

"I already have one," said Myriam meekly, pulling up her dress slightly to draw a small dagger attached to her slender calf. "It's just a knife really, I guess." She presented it to him. "My mother gave it to me three years ago. It is a Palaran custom to present a ceremonial dagger upon a girl's twelfth birthday, to symbolize her entering womanhood."

"It's beautiful," admired Ganry, taking it carefully from the Princess, turning it over and studying it. It was an elaborately decorated dagger, with precious stones and gems decorating the handle. The blade itself shone almost white as it caught the evening light that filled the room. He could tell it was made by a master. "Who forged this?"

"I'm not sure who made it, my mother never told me. She said it had been in her family for generations. She called it 'Harkan'. It came with this ring." Myriam held out her hand. Ganry examined the ring and noted that it was a perfect match for the knife. It was decorated in the same gems, shining with the same bright, white light.

"Keep these hidden," cautioned Ganry. "You shouldn't show anyone that you have them. It will only attract undue attention. Only draw the blade if your life depended on it." Ganry packed his weapons away and stored most of them under his bed for the night, tucking a simple dagger into his belt as a precautionary measure. "We'd better go downstairs and get some food before the kitchen closes," he said, leading the way. "Keep your cloak on, and try to remain discrete."

CHAPTER 2

Ganry and Myriam took a seat at one of the small tables in the bar. The innkeeper came over and took their orders. Venison stew was the only food available. Ganry ordered ale, and Myriam took small sips of watered wine. The only other patrons in the inn were three shady looking brutes sitting at the back, nursing tankards. They stared at Myriam, making her uncomfortable. She was glad of Ganry's rough appearance and muscular physique. They instinctively sensed that Ganry would not be easy pickings, so left them alone.

The food at the inn was surprisingly good, large chunks of meat in a thick gravy, served with a loaf of fresh bread. They both ate heartily, their stomachs reminding them that it had been a long time since their last meal, after a hard day of riding.

As they were eating a well-dressed young man entered the inn. He carried a longbow over his shoulder and looked like a nobleman. Ganry rested his hand on the hilt of his dagger, uneasy at the prospect that agents from Castle Villeroy may have tracked them down. The young nobleman took a seat at the bar and ordered some wine. He carried a large pouch of coins by his side, which did not escape the notice of the three brutes at the back. On closer inspection, Ganry sensed the young man was nervous and inexperienced, almost like he didn't belong in an inn like this. He was unlikely to be looking for them, but still Ganry still kept his guard up.

The largest of the brutes smacked his fist on table, making Myriam jump in surprise. "You seem a long way from home, little man," he said loudly, attracting the attention of the nobleman.

"Just passing through," replied the young man politely, sipping his wine at the other end of the bar from Ganry and Myriam.

"Do you have any spare coin for some honest woodsmen?" asked another of the men, getting up from their table and leaning next to the nobleman. This one was slimmer, with a hooked nose like a hawk. He had the type of smug face that Ganry just wanted to punch. "The least you could do is buy us a drink!"

They don't look anything like woodsmen. Woodsmen don't carry swords.

"Not today, sorry gentlemen," replied the nobleman, trying to sound firm but looking increasingly nervous.

"Oh, we're not gentlemen…" snarled the third brute, standing in an intimidating position behind the nobleman. This one was even uglier than hawk-nose, with a long scar along his jaw. "My friend here asked if you would be so kind as to buy us a drink. If you're going to be rude then we will have to show you exactly just who is in charge in these here woods!"

"You should help him," whispered Myriam to Ganry.

"Why? It's not our fight. You don't know who he is. He could be one of Duke Harald's men out looking for you."

"Give us your money!" shouted the largest brute, who was now standing threateningly in front of the nobleman. He grabbed the young man around the neck, tipping him off his stool, sending him crashing to the floor. He yanked the coin pouch, pocketing it, and they all began kicking the young man, stomping on him as he rolled around on the floor at their feet. They cheered each other on, laughing all the while.

"He looks familiar," whispered Myriam urgently. "I insist that you help him! Criminals should not have free rein in my father's kingdom. He would not have tolerated that."

Ganry reluctantly stood, drawing the attention of the men to him. "That's enough now, fellas. Take his gold and leave him be."

"Mind your business!" snarled the largest brute. He drew his knife, took a few steps forward and pointed it at Ganry's face. "Or you'll be next." He leered at Myriam sitting behind Ganry, her eyes wide in fear. She thought the brute looked a lot scarier now that he was closer, and directing his focus on her. She instantly regretted asking Ganry to help. There were three of them, and only one of him. The brute grabbed his crotch crudely. "And we'll have some fun with that sweet girl you've got hiding under that cloak."

"You asked for it." Ganry had held onto his tankard as he stood from the bar. While the large brute's attention was focused on Myriam, Ganry smashed his tankard over the brute's head, forcing him to reel back with a bloodied cranium, and drenched in ale.

Scar-jaw came running with his fist raised. Ganry kicked him in the knee, sending him sprawling to the ground in pain.

Hawk-nose drew his sword. "You bastard. I'm gonna slice and dice you, and then poke that bitch of yours until she screams for more."

In one quick motion Ganry stepped in to meet him, catching him with a straight left jab to his beak like nose, crushing it with satisfaction. "Let me give you some friendly advice," Ganry hissed, grabbing him by the throat. "A dagger is much better at close quarters. Here, let me demonstrate." Ganry drew his dagger, sticking hawk-nose in the stomach, dragging the blade up and out.

The large brute rushed at Ganry, who swiped his dagger in a horizontal arc, cutting the brute's face, drawing a howl of pain and anger. Ganry stomped on the hand of Scar-jaw, who was reaching for his own dagger. He thought about leaving it at that, but he didn't want to wake up in the middle of the night with large men looming over him, so he thrust his blade into Scar-jaw's neck, silencing him for good. Ganry pivoted immediately behind the large brute, quickly slitting his throat. He stepped towards Hawk-nose to finish him off, but he already lay in a pool of his own blood, his intestines spilled on the floor.

"What am I going to do with these bodies!" protested the innkeeper, emerging from behind the bar where he had been hiding.

"They're thieves," replied Ganry. "Probably rapists too. Bury them like thieves. Just don't put them in your stew."

"You didn't have to kill them!" exclaimed Myriam, helping the battered nobleman to his feet.

"I tried asking nicely," Ganry shrugged. "Men like that only respond to one thing."

"Princess Myriam?" asked the nobleman weakly, trying to focus on Myriam's face.

"Yes. Do I know you?"

"What are you doing?" growled Ganry. "Do not reveal your identity!"

"I know him. I think. Get some water for him, please." Ganry grudgingly fetched a pitcher of water and helped Myriam guide the injured man to their table.

"Thank you for your help." He sat down gingerly. "I am Artas," said the nobleman. "My father is Lord Holstein."

"Lord Holstein? I do know you! He is one of my father's closest allies!" exclaimed Myriam. "I remember you, Artas! What are you doing here?"

"When Duke Harald took control of Castle Villeroy, he arrested my father and all of my family. I only just managed to escape through the stables with my bow, and a small pouch of spare change." He looked around for his coin pouch. His bow was laying on the floor, miraculously undamaged in the brief scuffle.

Ganry unceremoniously flipped the large brute over, retrieving Artas's pouch, and dropped it on the table in front of him. The cord fell open and Ganry could see that it was filled to the brim with gold, more than he would earn in ten years. *Spare change, he called it.* Ganry rolled his eyes. Myriam grabbed the bow and handed it to Artas.

"Where will you go now?"

"I'm not sure, I just need to find somewhere safe until I can work out how to free my family."

"Ride with us!" Myriam suggested brightly. "We're headed for Castle Locke."

Ganry shook his head. "No, this is a really bad idea. He cannot ride with us. We probably have to kill him now that you have told him where we are going." He was only half-joking.

"Nonsense," dismissed the Princess. "Artas and I used to play together when we were children. His family have always been our most loyal supporters. He will travel with us and that is final. I will pay you more gold if that is what is required." Ganry grumbled unhappily, soothed a little by the prospect of more gold.

"We can't stay here tonight though. It's too dangerous. We'll have to get moving."

"Artas needs time to recover. Surely it is more dangerous for us to travel at night? Can we not stay until morning?" Ganry looked across at the innkeeper who was watching them intently. He walked over to speak with him at the bar.

"I'll help you dispose of these bodies," said Ganry, nodding towards the three dead 'woodsmen' that lay on the floor. "You can keep whatever they were carrying except for one horse, which I'll need. My young nobleman friend here will also leave you a generous tip, by way of an apology for causing such a commotion in your establishment. Do we have a deal?" The innkeeper nodded warily. Ganry knew that he was going to have to keep watch all night. This mission seemed to be becoming increasingly more difficult with each hour that passed.

CHAPTER 3

Ganry roused Myriam and Artas early the next morning so that they could continue their journey. As soon as the sun began to lighten the sky, they moved quickly away from the inn and the damage that they had left behind.

Artas slowed his horse to ride next to Myriam, leaving Ganry to ride a little ways ahead. He wanted a quiet word with the Princess of Palara.

"Princess, who is this man," Artas indicated with his head toward Ganry. "And are you sure you can trust him?"

"Please Artas, call me Myriam. No formalities. I don't know Ganry well, but my tutor Leonidavus vouched for him, and I trust Leonidavus. I'm not sure whether we can trust him though. Why don't we ask him?" Artas quickly shook his head, but Myriam smiled sweetly at him, and raised her voice. "Ganry! Artas wants to know if you are trustworthy."

Ganry turned in his saddle, placing his hand on his sword hilt. "You doubt my honor, boy?" he growled.

Artas raised his hands defensively. "I...no...of course not, never," he stammered.

Ganry harrumphed and turned back around, half grinning to himself.

Myriam stuck out her tongue at Artas.

She was in a bright mood as they continued to ride along the forest trail that followed the creek westward. "Does your horse have a name, Artas?"

"His name is Orton," smiled Artas weakly. He was still in pain from the night before, and also realized that Myriam had been having fun at his expense.

"He's beautiful!" admired Myriam. "Ganry's horse is called Bluebell. But I guess we don't know what this guy is called," she said, affectionately patting the neck of the horse that she was now riding, having liberated it from the dead 'woodsmen'. "I think I'll call you Oaken out of respect for your previous owner."

"No need to pay any respect to his previous owner!" laughed Ganry. "They were oafish brutes who would have happily killed us once they were finished with young Artas here."

"You can't hold Oaken responsible for that," protested Myriam. "Don't worry, Oaken," she said, ruffling the horse's mane. "I'll take care of you. We'll make a good team."

Artas smiled to himself. He couldn't help but be infected by Myriam's cheerful personality, though he was still worried about what lay ahead. "Do you know the forests of Cefinon well, Ganry?"

"No, this is not my country. The road is not safe for us though, so the forest is our best bet. As long as we keep heading west, then we are going in the right direction." They rode on in silence for a while, picking their way along the forest trail that followed alongside the creek. Ganry spotted a few hares running about, and pointed them out to both Myriam and Artas. "Are you good with that longbow, kid?"

"I'm lethal," grinned Artas.

"I'm not talking about hitting a target at archery practice. I'm talking shooting a moving object. Maybe even in an actual fight, a battle." Ganry wondered if he would be useful at all to have along. "Have you ever seen combat?"

"I have often won first place at royal tourneys."

"Somehow that doesn't fill me with confidence," said Ganry, shaking his head.

"Tell us about your sword, Ganry," interjected Myriam, looking for a way to change the subject. "How long have you had it?"

"A warrior's sword is a very personal thing." Ganry was always hesitant to discuss his long-sword. It was special, and rare. The types of qualities that made other men envious.

"My guess is you were a solider, or a knight of some kind," said Artas.

"Yes, a long time ago I served the Emperor Fontleroy. I led his legions into battle. This sword has kept me alive."

"Where did it come from? It's such an unusual design."

"It was forged by the Grimlock, high in the Limestone Mountains."

"My father has a Grimlock blade," said Artas. "He never talked much about it, except that it had a strange unpronounceable name. All Grimlock blades are apparently ancient. Was it created for you?"

"No, smart ass" said Ganry, shaking his head. He scratched at his growing beard. "I may seem old to you young-uns, but I'm not *that* old. This sword has been in our family for generations. It's name in the common-tongue, depending on the scholar you ask, translates to either *Wind* or *Storm*. I've always just called it Wind-Storm."

"I like it!" clapped Myriam.

The winding trail that they were following brought them within sight of a small wooden cabin, nestled in the forest.

"Wait here." Ganry dismounted from his horse and walked cautiously towards the cottage. He knocked at the door and after a few minutes it was opened by an elderly man. Myriam and Artas could see Ganry talking with him, eventually waving them forward. "We can eat here and refresh the horses."

The old man prepared a simple meal of bread and cheese. He had a long white beard and wore a strange looking conical hat. He was affable, generous with the food, and welcoming to the strangers. Myriam liked him instantly. He pottered around his small kitchen, bringing refreshments to the table. Myriam saw that his home was well-kept, though there were many strange jars. She wondered what they contained. Finally, the old man sat at the table and joined them.

"This is very kind of you," said Myriam, thanking the man as he tore the bread into pieces.

"It's nothing, child. We don't often get visitors as special as you," he said, his eyes sparkling.

"Oh, we're not special," deflected Myriam. "We're just traveling through, heading back to our farm."

"My dear girl, you've never set foot on a farm. And neither has your noble young friend here," he looked pointedly at Artas. "Well, you all seem a long way from home."

"You are very perceptive old man," cut in Ganry. "But enough questions, the less you know about our business the better."

"Indeed, these are troubled times…" nodded the old man sagely. "Kingdoms are in turmoil, and a princess has gone missing…"

Ganry and Myriam exchanged a worried look.

"Relax," the old man continued. "Who am I gong to tell?" His eyes sparkled. "In fact, I have a gift for you." From his pocket he pulled out a thin silver chain and held it out towards Myriam.

"Oh! It's beautiful," admired Myriam. "But honestly, I couldn't accept it, you really don't need to give us anything."

"Take it," insisted the old man. "Silver will help keep you pure and help ward off those that seek to harm you. Silver shimmers in the sun and shines in the light of the moon."

"It sounds like magic!" gasped Myriam as she allowed the old man to place the chain into the palm of her hand.

"Child, magic is a word that people use when they are unable to explain what they are seeing and feeling." The old man watched closely as Artas secured the chain around the neck of Myriam. "Objects can have power though, if we let them. If we believe in them."

"Thank you," said Myriam, tracing her fingers lightly along the silver chain that now hung around her neck.

"Time to go," announced Ganry firmly, standing up and preparing to leave.

"Safe travels children. My door is always open to you."

"You are too kind, thank you," said Myriam. "What is your name?"

"Barnaby," smiled the old man kindly, with a half bow. "I am known as Barnaby of Bravewood."

CHAPTER 4

"Do you think he is a wizard?" asked Myriam, looking back over her shoulder where Barnaby was watching them ride away.

"There's no such thing as wizards," scoffed Ganry.

"What do you think he meant by the power of this silver chain then?" Myriam ran the fine links of the chain between her fingers.

"He's just a lonely old man making up stories. Pay him no heed."

"Well I think it's all very mysterious. I like the idea of being a bit magical. It would be so much easier if I could simply cast a spell on uncle Harald and release my family from the dungeon." Tears began to roll down Myriam's cheeks at the thought of her family being held captive, possibly already dead.

"Hey... come on..." soothed Artas. "We have to stay strong. If we give up hope then there will be no chance of them being rescued."

"You're right, thanks Artas," said Myriam firmly, wiping the tears from her face. "Sorry. It just all got a bit too much for me for a moment there."

"Shhh!" hissed Ganry, pulling his horse to a stop. "Listen!" Artas and Myriam halted their horses and strained their ears to try and hear what had caught Ganry's attention.

"Is that dogs? Barking?" asked Artas, trying to catch the distant sound that seemed to be carried on the breeze.

"Hunting dogs," nodded Ganry.

"Hunters?" asked Myriam. "Do you think that they're hunting us?"

"It's hard to tell," replied Ganry. "We can't take any chances though."

"Do you think we're safe on this trail?" Artas shifted nervously on his horse. "Should we move deeper into the forest?"

"I don't really want to lose sight of this creek, or we might lose our bearings. I'm guessing that they're out near the road somewhere, but if they're looking for us then we have to expect that they'll start to push into the forest eventually."

"If we can't get to the road, where will we find shelter tonight?" asked Myriam.

"We'll have to camp out. Let's try and pick up the pace while we still have daylight, and then we can look for a clearing to make camp."

The three horses moved briskly along the forest trail, the travelers keeping any conversation to a minimum. They needed to stay alert for any sign that the hunters may be drawing closer, or that they were on their trail.

As the light of day began to dim and evening began to fall, Ganry found a clearing in the forest that seemed a suitable place for them to spend the night. Myriam secured the horses while Ganry built a fire. Artas soon returned with a couple of ducks that he had shot down by the creek.

"We'll have a feast in no time," smiled Ganry, pulling out one of his knives to begin preparing the ducks, skewering them onto a stick so that they could be roasted over the hot coals from the fire. "We'll need to set a watch. We'll take it turns," he said to Artas.

"I can take a turn too," volunteered Myriam.

"Okay," nodded Ganry. "That way we'll all get a few hours sleep."

"No Princess, you can't stand watch," objected Artas. "It's not right. I will take your watch for you."

"That's very sweet of you Artas, but we have a long journey ahead of us, and we all need to keep our strength up. I can take my turn on the watch. I promise that the minute a twig snaps or owl hoots then I will wake you both up." Artas reluctantly agreed and they focused on slicing off pieces of the roasting ducks.

Ganry took the first watch while Artas and Myriam slept. The forest was quiet. It was a still night, dark beneath the canopy of the trees, the stars hidden somewhere above. Ganry stared into the glowing embers of the fire, poking it gently with a stick to keep it burning. He was annoyed with himself for having got into this position, putting himself at risk in a fight that had nothing to do with him. He hated to admit it, but he felt protective of Myriam, the Princess of Palara. She was around the age that his own daughter would have been had she lived.

Ruby. His daughter's name had been Ruby. So full of life and love, Ganry felt sick at the memory of her loss, that she had been taken from him while still so young. He liked to think that Ruby would have been as strong and as independent as Myriam was proving to be. He had grown fond of Artas also. The young nobleman, so innocent and naive in the ways of the world, but with a strong sense of honor, duty, and loyalty. Despite his teasing, Ganry could see that Artas's bow skills were impressive.

He smiled wryly to himself. Here he was, an old worn out warrior, traipsing across the country trying to keep these two kids out of trouble. He pulled out his sword, WindStorm, and began to polish it gently, the light from the fire flickering in reflection along the blade, making it seem almost as if it were alight; a sword of flame, ready to burn it's enemies to ash.

Ganry returned WindStorm to its scabbard. There would be time enough for fighting, for battles, and for bringing enemies to justice. He always hoped that one day he would find peace, a quiet corner of the world where no one shouted for war, where no one was gripped by greed. Yet whenever he felt that he was getting close to that moment, something would drag him back into action, back into the fire.

CHAPTER 5

It was in deep in the night when Ganry woke Artas
to take his turn on the watch. Artas rubbed his eyes to
try and clear his head, propping himself up by the fire.
He had only slept fitfully, disturbed by dreams, his imagination fueled by the fear and uncertainty of the world
around him. Ganry wrapped himself in his cloak and
turned his back to the flames.

Artas looked across at the sleeping form of Myriam.
While they had played together as children, he had not
spoken to Myriam for years. They moved in different
circles and the life of a royal princess was sheltered and
protected - even from nobles such as himself. Getting to
know her better as they traveled on this journey, Artas
was forming a deep bond of affection for her, like a sister, reinforcing his loyal belief that she was the rightful
heir to the throne of Palara, and his commitment to
keeping her safe.

The fate of his own family continued to plague his
thoughts. Their arrest had been sudden and unforeseen.

It was difficult to know how brutal Duke Harald would be in eliminating the King and his supporters. All that Artas could do was to hope that they remained alive, to hope that somehow they would be reunited. The night went slowly by, Artas lost in his thoughts as he stared into the glowing embers of the fire.

A twig cracked in the darkness. Artas reached for his bow. Then silence. He remained alert, fearful that someone or something was watching them. The horses became restless. Their movement woke Ganry. Artas brought his fingers to his lips, indicating the need for silence.

"Do we have company?" whispered Ganry.

"I don't know," replied Artas quietly. There was a sound, then the horses became unsettled. Something is not right.

"Wake Myriam," instructed Ganry, firmly gripping the hilt of WindStorm. Artas gently placed his hand on Myriam's shoulder and she quickly stirred, heeding his signal to be quiet.

"It could be nothing," reflected Artas.

"It's better to be safe than sorry," said Ganry. The three travelers sat beside the fire, their backs to each other, peering out into the darkness. "What animals live in Cefinon Forest?" Ganry asked Artas as the night lay still around them.

"Deer mainly. There are some bears in the mountains."

"What about animals that would move at night?"

"Foxes. Occasionally wolves. Stoats and weasels. That kind of thing I guess."

"Yes… a fox would be curious enough to investigate us, before deciding that we were too big to bother with. Wolves would have moved quicker to attack the horses. Just to be on the safe side, let's all stay awake for the remainder of the night. Daybreak can't be too far away."

Eventually the morning sun's rays began to emerge through the gloom of the forest. They saddled up the horses and resumed the journey along the trail beside the creek. Artas couldn't shake the feeling that they weren't alone.

The sound of barking dogs broke through the stillness.

"Let's pick up the pace," urged Ganry. "They aren't on our tail, but those hunters are getting closer."

After several miles of hard riding, the trail that they were following led them towards a large house. Ganry pulled to a stop just on the edge of the clearing. "Who would live out here?"

"It looks like some sort of estate," observed Artas. "Should we just avoid it and keep going?"

"We could do with some grain for the horses as well as some food for ourselves," mused Ganry. "Why don't you go and see if you can find anyone, what sort of reception you get, and Myriam and I will remain concealed here. Do not reveal your identity, we have no idea where the loyalties of these people might lie." They watched as Artas slowly rode his horse Orton into the grounds of the estate and out of sight.

"Do you think those hunters are chasing us?" asked Myriam while they waited.

"We have to assume that they are," nodded Ganry. "If your uncle has put a bounty on your head then we have to assume that *everyone* is chasing us - even people that you may think are our friends. We've no idea how long your uncle has been planning this coup."

"I wish my father had talked with me more about the affairs of state," sighed Myriam. "Any time that I asked questions he said that I was too young and that he would tell me everything when I was older. I know a lot about romantic poetry and music, but not much else. Nothing that is of any use to us right now."

"You never know when you'll need some romantic poetry."

"Well with you two for companions I don't think I'll have any need in the near future!" laughed Myriam.

A few moments later Artas came riding back from the house.

"What did you find?" asked Ganry.

"It looks okay. This is a summer house for the Stapleton family. They're not here, but if we pay the foreman then we can refresh the horses and they will give us some supplies as well."

"Perfect. Lead the way."

They soon had their horses unsaddled. A table had been laid for them for lunch.

"So where are you heading?" asked the estate's foreman, joining them at their meal.

"West," replied Ganry, "back to our farm there."

"Unusual to be traveling along the old forest trail? Why don't you take the main road?"

"There seems to be a lot of soldiers on the road at the moment. We're simple folk. Easier to keep out of the way of trouble."

"You know… I had some hunters through here a day or so ago."

"Oh?" replied Ganry, biting into some bread and cheese, trying to appear disinterested.

"Yes, they were hunting some people. A man and a girl. They were offering a hefty reward for their capture. You wouldn't know anything about that would you?"

"Like I said, we're simple folk. We haven't heard anything about that."

"I've never seen a farmer carry a sword like that one," insisted the foreman.

"It's just a family heirloom. It's useful for deterring bandits. And people who ask too many questions." Ganry glared at him. He could tell the foreman would cause trouble. They would need to leave here sooner than they planned.

"I'm sorry sir," Myriam apologized to the foreman. "It's been a long journey for us and my father is tired and irritable. Please, tell me how much we owe you for your hospitality and we'll be on our way."

Artas handed over the payment and they quickly gathered up their horses and resumed their journey along the trail.

"You know that he's going to try and collect that ransom from the hunters. They'll be on our trail before nightfall," grumbled Ganry as the estate vanished into the trees behind them.

"I don't think your farmer story is particularly effective," said Artas. "None of us look like simple folk for starters. You are a warrior, and we are obviously noble."

"The farmer story is fine," Ganry insisted. "You just need to act more convincingly. Or why don't you come up with something better next time."

"Perhaps I will. Anyway, if they know that we're on this trail then their dogs will be able to track our scent whichever direction we go."

"The road is definitely too dangerous, we're going to need to push deeper into the forest. Let's take the horses into the water of the creek for a while, try and lose the scent."

They could only make slow progress but the horses tentatively picked their way along the narrow bed of the creek, dodging the loose stones and deep pot holes.

"There are fish swimming between the legs of the horses," observed Myriam. "Should we try and catch some?"

"Let's focus on getting somewhere safe first," cautioned Ganry. "We're going to need to find a camp within a few hours. It's going to be another long night without much sleep." The sound of barking dogs floated on the breeze that stirred through the leaves of the forest. "We need to stay in the water a bit longer, and then we'll try and find cover."

After another mile of slow progress through the water of the creek, they came to a small stone bridge where a young man was fishing. He looked up in surprise as the three travelers approached. Ganry placed his hand firmly on this hilt of his sword.

"Hello," said the young man cautiously.

"Hello," replied Artas.

"Why are you walking your horses in the water?" asked the young man. "You're scaring all the fish away."

"Sorry about that. We had just got a bit muddy on the path, a lazy way for us to clean their hooves."

"Oh," replied the young man, not particularly convinced.

"You live around here?" asked Ganry. The young man nodded. "What would we find if we rode that way?" Ganry pointed deeper into the forest.

"Why would you want to ride that way?" asked the young man perplexed. "There's nothing but forest. It just gets deeper and darker and then there's a big ravine. I don't know what's on the other side of the ravine, I haven't found a way across it yet. Wait a minute, you're hiding from those hunters aren't you?"

"Don't be silly," quipped Artas, looking sidelong at Ganry. "Can't you see we are just simple folk heading back to our farm? That sword and those blades that big man is carrying are all heirlooms. Myself and this young lady here, often enjoy dressing in our Sunday best while we toll the fields."

The young man just stared. "Err..."

"Artas!" laughed Myriam. "Yes, we're hiding from the hunters. Have they been past here?"

"Yes, a couple of times," nodded the young man. "I stay out of their way. Their dogs frighten the fish."

"Would you help us?" asked Myriam. "We need somewhere safe to spend the night."

The young man appeared to consider it. He had exchanged a few words with the hunters earlier. They claimed to be seeking a young servant girl who eloped with an older man. The young lady in front of him was definitely no servant, he knew that much. Her demeanor suggested one high-born. The young man claiming to be a farmer was dressed in fine, well cut clothes. He hesitated because of the large warrior glaring at him menacingly. But a smile and nod of encouragement from the pretty girl made up his mind.

"It would be my pleasure. My cottage is only small. But it's fairly well concealed. Follow me." The young man picked up his fishing rod and the string of fish that he had caught and led the way down a small narrow path. The three travelers followed, dismounting from their horses so that they could thread through the undergrowth and dodge the low hanging branches of the forest which immediately became denser on this side of the creek.

After about ten minutes of walking they came to a small clearing and a cottage made of logs and earth. There were a couple of goats tethered to a post and a handful of chickens scratching in the dirt. "Here we are!" said the young man proudly.

"You live here alone?" asked Myriam, noting that the cottage was particularly basic in every respect.

"Yes," replied the young man. "I lived here with my father, but he died last winter."

"I'm so sorry for your loss," said Myriam sadly, his words making her think of her own parents. "How rude of us, we don't even know your name. I'm Myriam, this is Artas, and that angry man is Ganry."

"Nice to meet you, I'm Hendon."

"I guess you don't get many visitors out here," observed Myriam. "Don't you get lonely?"

"I'm kind of used to it I suppose. I have the goats to keep me company. Will you share the fish that I caught?" Hendon proudly brandished the string of silvery brown trout.

"We would love to," beamed Myriam, happy to be welcomed by a friendly face.

Hendon set to work and expertly cleaned and prepared the fish, throwing some small logs onto the wood-burning stove so that he could heat a pan in which to fry them.

There weren't enough chairs around the small table, so Hendon graciously stood while his guests sat to eat. He was captivated by the young girl. He thought she looked like a living doll, as she was extremely pretty. But Hendon thought the young man, Artas, was even more arresting, with his handsome good looks.

"Hendon, could you guide us through the forest?"

Hendon started, afraid that Artas had caught him staring. "The only way to head further west is to cross the ravine. There's no way across."

"Are there no paths leading down into the ravine?" asked Ganry, picking at his teeth with a fish bone.

"Nothing that I've found. The sides are sheer, even the goats don't attempt it."

"What are we going to do?" moaned Artas. "It feels like we're trapped."

"Horses can swim, can't they?" asked Hendon. Ganry nodded. "About five miles downstream from here, the stream enters a large lake. If you could cross the lake you should then be able to pick up another trail that would lead you to the west."

"Sounds like a plan," said Ganry, getting up from his seat. "We'll leave tomorrow. I expect you to guide us to this lake, Hendon."

Hendon didn't feel like he was being given a choice. "Okay."

"Thank you Hendon," smiled Myriam brightly. "What about your goats and chickens?"

"My neighbor drops by occasionally. I'll leave him a note to care for them until I return."

Ganry stretched his arms wide and yawned. "We'd better get some sleep. It sounds like we've got a big day ahead of us tomorrow."

Hendon insisted that Myriam take his bed while he slept on the floor with Ganry and Artas. Myriam slept deeply, dreaming of her grandmother and Castle Locke.

CHAPTER 6

"You can ride with me," Artas offered to Hendon. "Orton is strong enough to carry both of us," he said, patting the neck of his horse. Hendon eagerly swung himself up to sit behind Artas. "Do we walk in the water of the creek again or risk taking the trail?"

"We'll move much quicker on the trail," decided Ganry. "We'll just have to hope that the hunters are behind us and not ahead of us. Let's go."

Hendon and Artas led the way along the winding forest trail, snaking its way through the trees beside the crystal clear waters of the creek.

"Isn't it dangerous? Living in the forest by yourself?" Myriam asked Hendon.

"Dangerous? What could harm me out here?"

"Oh, I don't know, bears… wolves… woodsmen…" suggested Myriam.

"It's more dangerous living in a castle by the sound of it."

"You have a point," sighed Myriam. "Maybe I would be better off living out here in the forest."

The sound of barking dogs cut through their conversation.

"They're close!" snarled Ganry, urging his horse into a fast canter. "How far to the lake?" he shouted to Hendon.

"Just a few more miles!" Hendon was clutching onto Artas to avoid falling off as they sped along the uneven track.

Artas rode up beside Ganry. "Sounds like they're out on the road." Another bout of barking suggested otherwise. "And behind us! We could have two packs on our tail!"

"They know we're heading west. They must be covering every escape route possible. Let's just hope that they haven't thought of the lake. You go on ahead with Myriam. I'll try and distract them and buy us some time!"

"Are you sure?" shouted Artas.

"Yes, go!" urged Ganry, pulling his horse Bluebell to a standstill and watching Artas and the others ride on towards the lake. The sound of barking dogs was drawing closer. Ganry quickly tried to think of a way that he could slow down the hunters that were in pursuit.

Meanwhile Artas and Myriam drew within sight of the lake.

"Let's aim for that rock over there on the other side," pointed out Artas. "We can't swim too far or the horses will tire. Try and keep the heavy cloaks dry by tying them on top of the saddle. We'll need to swim with the horses to lead them. Quickly now!" Myriam followed

Artas's instructions, preparing Oaken to go into the water while Artas tied his cloak on to Orton's saddle.

Myriam looked around in alarm. "Where's Ganry?"

"He'll be here," reassured Artas. "Get going now, start swimming. They may chase us into the water."

"Hendon! You should come with us," Myriam waved her hand urgently, beckoning him. "If the hunters catch you, who knows what they will do to you."

"I can't! I have to stay!" protested Hendon.

"It's too dangerous!" insisted Myriam. "At least help me swim Oaken to the other side!" Hendon relented and helped Myriam lead her horse into the water. They tentatively began to swim across the lake, leading Oaken towards the rock on the opposite shore. Artas looked hopefully down the track, trying to see some sign of Ganry. All of the sudden there came loud yelling.

"Artas! Your bow!" Ganry was riding recklessly down the narrow winding forest trail, as fast as he could possibly go. "The dogs! Shoot the dogs!"

Artas knelt one knee to the ground to steady his aim. He notched his first arrow and waited for a clean shot. As Ganry rounded the final bend, Artas could see a pack of large wolf-hounds almost upon him, barking, snarling, snapping at Bluebell's hooves as he galloped along in panic. Artas released his first arrow and one of the dogs fell down. He calmly notched a second arrow and released it. Another dog fell. He could see that Ganry was also being pursued by men on horses. He contemplated targeting them but decided to follow Ganry's instructions and loosed his third arrow to take down another dog. His fourth arrow and fifth arrow both missed. His sixth arrow finally felled the last wolfhound just as Ganry skidded to a halt next to Artas at the edge of the lake.

Artas watched in amazement as Ganry spun Bluebell around on the spot and rode straight at the pursuing hunters. Drawing a wicked looking curved short-sword in his left hand, and his long sword in his right, he swung the blades with a mad fury that made the hunters hesitate in their attack. His long sword, WindStorm was just a blur, creating a high pitched whooshing sound as it cleaved through the air. *Just like the wind.*

Artas considered shooting his bow, but with Ganry in amongst the hunters he didn't want to risk it. It didn't look like Ganry needed help in any case. In a few short moments, all four hunters had been cleanly dispatched. Artas saw that Bluebell was instrumental in the victory, using his body to barge into the other horses, knocking the men off balance. Ganry used his short blade to block, and WindStorm to thrust up close. He would swing the blade in big arcs to parry and cleave at a distance. As the last of the huntsmen fell from his horse, Ganry raised his sword high in the air and shouted in triumph at the empty forest.

"Ganry, we need to go!" urged Artas, securing his bow and cloak to the saddle of his horse, Orton, and leading him into the lake. "There are bound to be more huntsmen on our trail. We should keep moving."

"Of course, you're right. Sometimes the rush of battle overwhelms me." Ganry quickly secured his cloak and sword to the saddle of the panting Bluebell and followed Artas into the water. They could see that

Myriam and Hendon were almost half way across the lake, making good progress towards the rock they were aiming for.

"Nothing in this lake that we need to worry about?" shouted Ganry to Artas as they led their horses, swimming through the water.

"Such as what?"

"I don't know… we never swam in the marshes of Llandaff because of the snakes there… just wondering if there was anything that I should be keeping an eye out for."

"I think the catfish grow pretty big around here but let's just get to dry land and try not to think about it." Artas increased the speed of his swimming.

When they reached the other side of the lake, Hendon and Myriam helped to pull them up out of the water.

"Can we light a fire and try to keep warm?" asked Myriam.

"Given the mess that we've just left on the other side of the lake, I don't think it would be wise to hang around. We should get moving," said Ganry, trying to shake the water out of his pants. "Lead the way Hendon."

"I can't go with you. I can't leave my home," protested Hendon.

"Hendon, there's a whole world waiting out there for you. You've proven yourself useful. Look, Myriam is the princess of Palara. Serve your kingdom, boy. She needs you more than your goats and chickens."

Hendon stood flabbergasted. He decided to drop to one knee. He heard that's what people do in the presence of royalty.

"Oh get up," Ganry pulled him to his feet. "No time for that. You might not have been this way before, but you know the forest better than we do, so lead the way." He gave Hendon a little push in the back. "That's not a suggestion."

Myriam tried to smooth the situation. "Please be nice, Ganry. Here Hendon, you can ride with me for a while."

Hendon sighed, resigned to his predicament. He swung himself up behind Myriam, on the back of Oaken. "It's this way," he pointed.

They rode mostly in silence, each lost in their own thoughts. It was a warm day, and as they rode, their clothes soon began to dry.

"Are you okay?" asked Artas, falling back a little to ride next to Ganry.

"Yes, that was a close one. Thanks for your help back there. I didn't stand a chance with those dogs on my heels. That's some nice shooting. I knew it was a good idea to bring you along."

"That's not how I remember it," chuckled Artas.

"Does this forest run all the way to the Berghein Valley?" Myriam asked Hendon.

"I'm not really sure," replied Hendon. "I haven't been this far before. But we're traveling west so that's the right direction at least, isn't it?"

"Yes I guess so. I suppose there's nothing stopping the hunters swimming across the lake too, but I feel that we've at least got a bit of a head start on them. I just wish we knew what lay ahead."

"I can't help you with that one I'm afraid, fortune telling has never been one of my strengths. You need Barnaby of Bravewood for that."

"Barnaby?" Myriam touched the silver chain that hung around her neck. "You know him?"

"Yes of course," nodded Hendon. "Everyone in the Cefinon Forest knows Barnaby."

"He gave us food as we rode past his cottage. He gave me this nice little present. Are you saying he is a fortune teller?"

"There's not much that Barnaby can't do. At least that's what he says. My father always warned me to stay away from him, saying that he practiced dark arts, but I've always found him fairly harmless. I like the stories he tells."

"What sort of stories?"

"Stories about the forest and the kingdom mostly. Sometimes wilder stories of what the future might hold."

"And what did he tell you that your future would hold?" probed Myriam.

"He said that I would meet a Princess and be swept away on an adventure."

"Really?" gasped Myriam.

"No, I'm only joking," laughed Hendon. "But he did say that silver will help ward off those that seek to harm you. Silver shimmers in the sun and shines in the light of the moon. He gave me one of those chains too."

"We seem to be matching our jewelery well!" clapped Myriam. "This forest is full of surprises."

The travelers followed the forest trail quietly for several hours until Ganry called them to a halt. "I can see smoke up ahead."

"It could be the town of Athaca," said Hendon. "I've heard that it's somewhere here in the forest."

Myriam tried to peer through the trees for signs of civilization. "Why would a town be all the way out here?"

"I think they log trees and then float them down the river to the port of Brammanville."

"That could be handy if we wanted to go north," mused Ganry. "But it doesn't help us get west. The question is whether we go in or whether we try and keep a low profile and go around."

"I don't think we can go around," noted Artas, pointing at the ground. "It looks like this trail goes straight into the town. It's bordered by the river on one side and thick forest on the other."

"Ride ahead Artas, see what you can find out," suggested Ganry. "We'll wait here for you."

"Won't we be fairly conspicuous if we rode into town?" asked Myriam.

"We may not have any option. Let's see what Artas can find out."

"So sad that they are cutting down the trees," said Hendon quietly, watching the smoke drift lazily into the sky.

Myriam followed his gaze. "I guess they need them to build the boats though."

"It hurts the forest," Hendon said sadly.

"But can't the trees grow back?"

"Barnaby says that new trees can grow, yes, but once a tree is cut down it dies, it's spirit dies. He said that if you anger the forest then it will remember the pain that you have caused it. That the forest never forgets."

"That's a bit creepy isn't it?" said Myriam, eyeing the trees around her slightly more circumspectly.

They waited about an hour before Artas finally rode back into their little makeshift resting place.

"So what's the verdict?" Ganry asked Artas as he walked his horse towards them.

"We definitely have to go through. It would take us days to try and work our way around. Unless you want go up across the mountain, there's no way that we'd be able to cross the river unless we go over the town's bridge."

"What's the town like? How conspicuous will we be?"

"Hendon was right, it's a logging town. But there seemed to be quite a few merchants and other travelers passing through, so if we keep a low profile we should be okay. There's an inn not far from the gate that this trail will take us to. We could spend the night there until we get a better sense of the terrain that lies ahead of us."

"Good work. Let's do it," accepted Ganry. "Lead on Artas, we'll follow."

CHAPTER 7

Athaca was only a relatively small town. It was walled on all sides except where it faced the river. The River Walsall was one of the major waterways in the Kingdom of Palara, beginning high in the Basalt mountains, and flowing through the Cefinon Forest before reaching the Damatine Sea where the port of Brammanville had been built. The walls protecting Athaca were not made of stone, but of wood, from trees that had been felled from the forest. The gate that serviced the forest trail was relatively small, but it was manned by the town guard.

"What's your business in Athaca?" demanded the guard as Ganry presented himself.

"We are returning to our farm in the west," replied Ganry. "We seek lodging in Athaca for the night."

"Not the farm again," whispered Artas under his breath.

"Shut up," Ganry hissed back, while smiling politely at the guard.

The guard looked at them suspiciously. He eventually produced a ledger. "Write your name in this book. We are to record all entrances and exits." Ganry quickly made up names for them all and entered them into the book. "Any weapons to declare?" asked the guard.

"No," replied Ganry, pulling his cloak tighter around him to conceal the sheath of his sword. "Just my son's hunting bow."

"Very well, carry on," nodded the guard, opening the gate for them.

"I wrote our names as the Johannson family," Ganry whispered to Artas. "We need to make sure that we use the same name when we ask for the room at the inn."

"No problem... dad."

"Shut up fool," grinned Ganry.

The inn was fairly small and basic but they were able to secure a room that would sleep them all. Hendon and Myriam took charge of the horses while Ganry and Artas investigated the town.

"Look at that, Artas. How industrious." Ganry watched the industrious woodmen of Athaca at work. They were dragging the wood in from the forest, and then tipping the logs into the river to send it downstream.

"How do they stop it from getting caught in a log-jam along the way?" wondered Artas aloud.

"I guess they have checkpoints of some kind along the river, plus they probably send men down on rafts to help clear any blockages."

"They seem to be sending a lot of logs down. Do you think they're building a lot of boats?"

"It could be that," considered Ganry. "Perhaps some houses too? But mainly boats I imagine. Duke Harald is likely increasing the size of his fleet."

They walked on through the town and found the main gate that they would need to leave through in the morning in order to continue their journey westward.

"How are we going to get through that?" asked Artas, studying the heavily guarded gate.

"We'll just have to hope that they accept that we're the Johansson family and that they don't ask us too many questions."

"Isn't that fairly risky?"

"No more risky than walking in like we've just done," countered Ganry.

They returned to the inn and met up with Myriam, who was just about to go look for them.

"Should we try and buy another horse for Hendon?"

Ganry stood at the window looking down onto the busy street below. "Yes, probably a good idea. We'll be able to move faster if we've each got a horse. Artas, take Hendon with you and go and buy one."

Once Artas and Hendon left the room, Myriam sat down on the bed. She looked exhausted.

"How are you holding up?" asked Ganry.

"I'm okay," she smiled weakly. "Just tired I guess. This feels like the first time we've stopped since my world was turned upside down. If I don't think about what we're running from or what we're heading to then I'm fine, I can focus on just surviving. But I'm scared Ganry... I'm really scared."

Ganry didn't want to patronize her by saying things would be fine. He just patted her shoulder comfortingly.

"Perhaps we should send word to your grandmother. Let her know that you're coming and what has happened."

"Who could we trust with such a message, Ganry? I think we're better just to keep going, get there as soon as we can." Myriam sighed. "How far do we still have to travel?"

"If we were on the road it would take us another eight days, but we can't risk that. Once they realize that we evaded the hunters they'll increase their efforts to find us. We're going to have to work our way along the trails of the Cefinon Forest, so it's anyone's guess really."

Myriam flopped back onto her bed, and tried to get some rest.

CHAPTER 8

Duke Harald sat brooding, alone in the throne room of Castle Villeroy. He had an important decision to make. King Ludwig and his wife Queen Alissia were safely locked away in the dungeons of the castle. The plan had been to kill them immediately and claim the throne, but the escape of the Princess Myriam complicated things.

Myriam was the legitimate heir to the throne, and while she lived, Harald's right to rule would always be under threat. It infuriated him that she continued to evade capture. Duke Harald's dilemma was whether to kill the King now and claim the throne immediately or to continue to wait and delay any action until Myriam had been captured. Regicide is no small matter. To kill a king is a bold decision - especially when the king is your brother.

Duke Harald's ambitions to seize the throne had been brewing for a very long time. He had always been the stronger of the two brothers, the more aggressive. It was Harald that had led the armies, seen to the defense of the Kingdom of Palara, and commissioned the expansion of the Kingdom's fleet of ships. It was a cruel twist of fate that he was the younger of the brothers, that it was Ludwig that had been crowned King. That Ludwig had borne a child was yet another obstacle for Harald to overcome.

He tugged at his beard in frustration, trying to decide what to do, and the best course of action.

"Excuse me, sir," said a tentative voice, as the door to the throne room slowly opened.

"Yes, what is it?" responded Harald gruffly.

It was Henrickson, his captain of the guard. "We've had a report from the hunting party that was pursuing Myriam."

"And?" demanded Harald impatiently.

"We're not exactly sure what happened but she has eluded them, sir."

"What do you mean, eluded them?" growled Harald. "She is a fifteen year old girl. How has she possibly eluded a hunting party?"

"She must be under the protection of someone, sir," suggested Henrickson. "Half the hunters were slain, the dogs too. No fifteen year old girl could have done that."

"So there *was* someone with her when she escaped," snarled Harald. "I knew it. But you found the body of her tutor?" Henrickson nodded. "So there are other agents at work," reflected Harald. "Where did the hunting party lose sight of her?"

"They were deep in the Cefinon Forest. It appears that she crossed Lake Braff, heading West."

"They are in pursuit?"

Henrickson nodded. "Yes sir, they are heading towards the logging town of Athaca. We have sent reinforcements there also."

"Tedious little witch!" spat Harald. "It infuriates me that we are wasting time scouring the Kingdom for this girl. Carry on Henrickson. Bring her to me as soon as she is captured. Kill anyone that is trying to protect her."

Henrickson bowed and left the room.

Harald started to pace. He always did this when trying to calm himself. He was angry that one young girl could thwart his carefully laid plans. Whoever was helping her would pay dearly.

Harald had always been an ambitious man. His father had taught him well. Harald had been schooled in the art of war from a young age - how to fight, how to kill, how to plan a battle, and how to defend a city. Frustratingly he had been born into a long, extended period of peace for the Kingdom of Palara. There was the odd border skirmish, the occasional pursuit of a marauding gang of bandits, but on the whole there were few threats to the security of the kingdom. Diplomacy and trade became the weapons of choice while he gnashed his teeth and sharpened his sword.

He'd never had any interest in taking a wife. Women bored him. He dreamed of power. He dreamed of control. The plan to overthrow the rule of his brother Ludwig began to germinate and grow in his imagination when he was twenty-one. On a dare from one of his men, Harald had consulted a fortune teller. She was a wizened old woman draped in a shawl and burning incense to try and conceal her stench.

"You dream of glory..." croaked the old woman, studying Harald's hand. "But yet you will die alone. You will die alone and your dreams will crumble to dust..." Harald had been so enraged by the old woman's prophecy that he had drawn his sword and slit her throat. He was determined that fate would not decide his destiny, that he would make his dreams come true, and that he would be the most powerful man that the world had ever seen. His name would be remembered throughout history.

At first he had tried reasoning with his brother, Ludwig. Explaining the importance of building a strong army and expanding the influence and control of the Kingdom of Palara. He elaborated in detail on the need to build stronger alliances and subjugate those that refused to cooperate. But Ludwig was too content, too comfortable to see and understand what was possible, and what could be achieved. He wanted peace, but all that Harald dreamed of was war.

On his deathbed their father had arranged Ludwig's marriage to Alissia from the House of Locke. Harald had never really understood their father's fascination with Castle Locke, but Alissia had proved to be a loyal wife to Ludwig. Soon after they were married, Myriam had been born and the succession of the throne secured.

Ludwig and Alissia had to die, of that Harald was certain, but he knew that he couldn't kill them while Myriam lived. He needed to finish this cleanly, once and for all. Ludwig and Alissia would have to remain in the dungeon until Myriam was captured. Until Myriam could be brought back in chains.

CHAPTER 9

King Ludwig had been content to let his brother Harald assume leadership of the armies of the Kingdom of Palara. Ludwig's interests lay more in the negotiation of trading agreements with their neighbors. The rough and tumble of the army was more suited to the temperament of his hot headed brother.

Under the stewardship of Duke Harald, the armies of the Kingdom of Palara had almost doubled in size. He had transformed it from being a part-time military made up of conscripted farmers and tradesmen, into a professional army of men trained to fight, equipped with swords, shields, and armor.

They may have lived in a time of peace, but for many years the armies of the Kingdom of Palara had been preparing for war. A war that King Ludwig had not seen coming.

While Castle Villeroy was well protected by its defenses and a detachment of the Royal Guard, Duke Harald had developed two other centers of military power. The Walbourg Fort and the The Port of Brammanville.

The Walbourg Fort was located on a rocky outcrop that overlooked the river Walsall, downstream from the logging town of Athaca. It was here that Duke Harald had created an enormous armory for the Kingdom and had built barracks to house the thousands of professional soldiers that he had recruited and trained. The Fort was in a strategic position, controlling any traffic on the river, looking out across the lower plains and out to the Damatine Sea. Soldiers could move quickly on horseback or could be transported by river raft down to Brammanville.

Brammanville had long been an important port for the Kingdom of Palara. A bustling trade hub that had taken Palara's grains and produce across the Damatine Sea to their trading partners in the cold lands of the north.

Shipbuilding had been a skill and tradition that the men of Brammanville prided themselves on. Their trading ships were wide and flat, enabling them to make long-distance journeys across the Damatine Sea, but also to cope with the narrow waters of the Marshes of Llandaff and other inland water-ways. But Duke Harald wanted a different kind of ship. He wanted ships that could carry the Kingdom's soldiers and horses. Ships that carry the Kingdom to war and carry the Kingdom to victory.

Unbeknown to Ludwig, Harald embarked on a massive ship building program, creating a fleet that was now safely anchored in the harbor of Brammanville. A fleet of ships ready for a war that had not yet been de-clared, against enemies that had not yet been identified.

CHAPTER 10

"Henrickson!" shouted Duke Harald.

"Yes sir," replied the Harald's captain of the guard, entering the throne room of Castle Villeroy.

"If we assume that we will soon have dealt with the inconvenient Princess and my brother, we need to start planning our next move," said Harald.

"Yes sir," nodded Henrickson. "I have prepared a map room where you can consider how you would like to mount the campaign."

"Excellent," nodded Harald, following his captain to the adjacent room. Henrickson had set up a table with a large map of the region. The Kingdom of Palara was shown in the center. To the east the hilly lands controlled by the tribes of Ashfield and beyond that the plains of Mirnee. To the south the Basalt Mountains and the lands controlled by the Hartnett family. To the west the Berghein valley and the House of Locke. "What I'm interested in is here..." said Harald, pointing to the north-west.

"Vandemland?"

"Yes…" mused Harald. "They've never responded to any of our trade delegations. We share a land border with them but they keep it well fortified, and from what I hear their mines are producing valuable seams of metals and jewels."

"They have always been fiercely independent. It is difficult to gauge their military capabilities. We don't even have very good maps of what lies within their borders."

"We have two points of access though. There is the land border that we share with them, but they also have an extensive coastline along the Damatine Sea. We could use our ships to launch an attack on two fronts," said Harald, using the map to illustrate his plans.

"But what would our objective be, sir?" asked Henrickson.

"To conquer Vandemland and subjugate it to the rule of Palara," said Harald firmly. "Imagine what message that would send to our neighbors. Not only would we take control of Vandemland's mines but we would also show our strength and determination to the world around us."

"If we launch an attack against Vandemland do we not leave ourselves exposed?"

"It is a point well made," concurred Harald. "We will need to secure our borders, but we have no existing quarrels with anyone. They will not be expecting us to move against Vandemland. But we cannot move until Myriam has been captured and executed along with my brother."

"We could send spies into Vandemland to try and assess their strength and assist our planning?"

"Yes, excellent Henrickson," agreed Harald. "Better yet, why don't you go?"

"Me, sir?" asked Henrickson in surprise.

"Yes. It is a mission too sensitive to entrust to anyone else. You will be the one leading our forces in the attack so it makes sense for you to see how the territory lies in these lands to the north-west. Take a few men with you, and leave tomorrow. I will take care of disposing of my brother and his daughter while you continue our plans for war."

"Of course sir, as you wish. When would you like me to report back?"

"As soon as possible. Our soldiers are ready. Our fleet of ships is ready. Our nation is ready for war. We just need to dispose of my brother. Once I am King of Palara our nation marches!"

CHAPTER 11

Back in the logging town of Athaca, on the River Walsall, Artas and Hendon was on their way to buy a horse that Hendon could ride on their journey to Castle Locke. Artas had asked the innkeeper for directions on where the best place to buy a horse would be, and the innkeeper had suggested that they try the farrier near the western gate. As they approached, Artas could see that the farrier was busy at work, preparing a new pair of shoes for a horse that was tethered nearby.

"Good day!" greeted Artas politely. The farrier barely acknowledged their presence. "We were told that you might have horses for sale?"

"Who wants to know?" growled the farrier.

"We are traveling to the west, returning to our farm there. One of our party needs a horse for the journey."

"Those three are for sale over there," grumbled the farrier, pointing to the stables at the back of the farrier's premises. Artas and Hendon went to look at the three horses. They didn't seem to be particularly well-cared for and none of them were in great condition. "Well these aren't particularly inspiring," said Artas quietly to Hendon. "What do you think, should we look elsewhere in town?"

"Shhh, don't be so hasty," smiled Hendon, stepping forward and running his fingers through the mane of the closest horse. "You'll hurt their feelings. These are all fine horses. They just need a bit of love and affection."

"Okay..." Artas said skeptically. "I'm sorry if I hurt their feelings. So which one of these fine animals would you like to carry you to the Berghein Valley?"

"I would like to take them all. They're not happy here."

"You can only have one, Hendon." Artas crossed his arms. "Come on now, which will it be?"

Hendon placed his arm around the neck of the middle horse. "This one. He has been to the west before, he knows the way."

Artas rolled his eyes. "Whatever you say, Hendon." Artas quickly negotiated the sale with the farrier and they were soon leading their new purchase back to the inn where Ganry and Myriam were waiting. "Oh, we forgot to ask the farrier what the horse's name is!" said Artas, stopping suddenly, thinking that they would have to turn around and go back to get this information.

"Don't worry, it's okay, I know it," said Hendon cryptically.

"What do you mean? How do you know it?"

"Well, it's just a hunch I have," shrugged Hendon.

"So, what does your hunch tell you? What's the horse's name?"

"Bartok," replied Hendon confidently.

"If you say so," said Artas, raising an eyebrow.

They were soon back at the inn and Hendon was making Bartok at home in the stables, ensuring that he had plenty of feed and water, brushing his coat thoroughly, and adjusting the saddle that they had purchased from the farrier.

"This was the best that you could find?" quizzed Ganry, emerging from the inn to see how they had got on.

"Shhh... you'll hurt the horse's feelings," quipped Artas.

"Eh?"

"Looks can be deceiving," said Hendon. "But this is Bartok. He is a clever horse, lots of stamina, nothing will startle him."

"Come on, I'm getting hungry. Let's have some dinner."

Artas and Hendon finished up in the stables and joined Ganry and Myriam at a small table in the corner of the bar. The inn-keeper came over and took their meal order. There wasn't a lot of choice. A meat stew or some pork sausages. Ganry noticed that Hendon was pushing his food around his plate, looking quiet and thoughtful.

"You must be missing the fish from your creek?"

"I am," nodded Hendon. "And my goats and my chickens. I miss the forest."

"I'm sorry Hendon," said Myriam gently, placing her hand lightly on his arm. "I know it must feel that we dragged you away from your home. I guess we did in a way, but I don't think it was safe for you there any more, because of us more than anything. I'm sorry that we made you come with us, but I'm really glad that you did. I'm really glad that you're here."

"It's okay. My father always said that I would have to leave the forest at some stage."

"Why did he say that?" asked Ganry.

"I'm not really sure. He never explained it. Sometimes he would say that there were forces beyond the forest that were greater than all of us, and that at some stage our past would catch up with us."

"I wonder what he meant by that?" pondered Myriam.

Ganry finished up the last of his sausage. "And how did your father die?"

"He was old..." replied Hendon, looking down at the table. "His body was weak, he had injuries, scars. One cold winter's day he just didn't wake up, the cold night had taken him. I shook his body, tried to stir him, tried to call him back, but it was too late. He was gone and I was on my own."

"Well you're not on your own now," said Myriam, trying to comfort him. "We may not be family but we are your friends. Who knows what we'll find on our journey to the west. Maybe you'll discover something about yourself that will surprise you."

CHAPTER 12

"Right! Let's get moving!" said Ganry loudly, rousing his traveling companions out of their beds. "Let's make an early start and get on the road!" Myriam, Artas, and Hendon all soon pulled themselves out of their small narrow beds and prepared for departure. The horses were saddled and their rucksacks packed with supplies. "Remember, when we get to the main gate they will want to check us off their list. We entered Athaca as the Johansson family, we're heading west back to our farm. Okay?"

"What happens if they challenge us?" asked Artas.

"We'll just have to play that by ear if it happens. We know that the gate will be heavily guarded. We know that they're checking everyone in and out. If we run into any trouble we're not going to be able to fight our way out of it, we just need to stick to our story. We're the Johansson family, we're farmers. Nothing more." They mounted their horses and Ganry led the way on Bluebell.

When they reached the main gate of Athaca, there seemed to be a lot of activity and commotion.

"This doesn't look good," said Artas quietly. They pulled their horses to a standstill to try and get a handle on what was happening. "Do we push on and try and get through?"

"What's going on?" shouted Ganry to a merchant who seemed to be returning from the direction of the gate.

"They've shut the gate!" replied the merchant. "They've arrested someone."

"Damn," cursed Ganry under his breath. "Hold my horse," he said, handing Bluebell's reins to Artas. "I'll go and see what I can find out." Ganry pushed through the crowd so that he could get a view of what was happening at the gate. There were a lot of soldiers everywhere and a growing crowd of people wanting to use the gate to exit the city. Craning his neck, Ganry could see that a group of soldiers were holding a man, his hands tied behind his back. The crowd were jeering, jostling for position as the soldiers seemed to be waiting for instructions on what to do. "Why have they arrested him?" asked Ganry, turning to one of the onlookers.

"He's been accused of practicing the dark arts," replied the onlooker. Ganry looked again - the man looked familiar. Suddenly it hit him. The man that had been arrested was Barnaby of Bravewood.

Ganry quickly returned to his traveling companions and relayed the news of his discovery.

"We have to save him," said Myriam firmly.

"We can't save everyone," hissed Ganry, concerned that they were becoming more vulnerable with every minute they remained in Athaca.

"I'm not leaving while Barnaby is being held captive here," added Hendon flatly.

"Ganry, it's obvious that he's been arrested because they suspect him of helping us," added Myriam. "The hunters would have been able to follow our trail right to his door."

"All the more reason for us not to interfere," insisted Ganry. "They're probably using him as a decoy to get us to reveal ourselves in some sort of foolish rescue attempt! You have no idea how many soldiers are manning that gate. They clearly know that we're here. The next thing will be a door-to-door search. We have to get out of here!"

"Well, as the gates are closed there's not much prospect of that at the moment though, is there?" added Artas. "Hypothetically, if we were to try and rescue Barnaby, how might we go about it?"

"I'm not even entering into this discussion," replied Ganry. "If we make any attempt to rescue Barnaby it will get us all killed. It is highly likely that we will all be killed anyway. We never should have entered Athaca."

"We had no choice, Ganry," reminded Myriam. "And if we are all going to die anyway then we may as well die trying to rescue Barnaby."

"So that's settled then? You're making all the decisions now?" said Ganry, raising an eyebrow.

"What if we caused some sort of distraction," suggested Artas. "Like setting one of their boats on fire?"

"No, it has to be bigger than that," replied Ganry. "We have to set the wall on fire, draw the soldiers away from the gate."

"So you do have a plan!" smiled Myriam. "I knew you wouldn't let us down."

"I need my head read," grumbled Ganry. "Artas, take Hendon, find a secluded part of the wall where you can work without drawing too much attention to yourself. The walls are made from forest timbers but they won't burn easily - they've treated the beams to make them as tough as possible. You're going to have to create some sort of fire trap, build it with straw and wood but you'll also need some sort of fuel like oil if the fire is to catch hold and threaten the wall. It needs to look like a big fire, even if it's not doing that much actual damage.

"Princess, you and I will focus on Barnaby. Once we see the flames taking hold, you need to try and distract the crowd, draw their attention to the flames, whip up some panic, I'll move in and kill anyone that stands between me and Barnaby. We meet back here, grab our horses and then push through the main gate dispatching anyone or anything that stands in our way. Is everyone clear?" They all nodded.

Ganry was not feeling nearly as confident as he was sounding. "Right, let's go. Artas and Hendon, you have fifteen minutes to get that blaze going. Once it is burning, get back to the horses. Princess, don't draw too much attention to yourself, just generate a bit of panic and make sure everyone sees that there is a fire threatening the wall. This is our only chance to get out of Athaca. Let's do our best to avoid the dungeons of Castle Villeroy."

CHAPTER 13

"Fire! Fire!" screamed Myriam, as soon as she saw the flames and smoke emerging above the roofs of the buildings near the town's walls. Myriam had pushed herself into the middle of the frustrated crowd that was waiting for the gates of Athaca to open. Her screaming quickly drew attention and concern as everyone craned their necks to see the fire. The smoke was now billowing in dark clouds.

The soldiers manning the gate tried to keep order, dispatching several men to investigate. Myriam was growing concerned that she wasn't getting much movement from the crowd, despite her loud hysterical screaming. If she couldn't create some panic then they wouldn't be able to get past the guards that were holding the gate closed.

"Dragon!" screamed Myriam hysterically. "Oh my god, I think I saw a dragon! We're under attack from a dragon!" Fortuitously, just at the point, the fire seemed to catch on to some straw and light timber and burst up the wall, high above the roof tops of the buildings. The crowd of people tried to move, looking to get further away from the fire, away from the screaming girl. The more the soldiers tried to keep everyone contained in the area near the gate, the more restless the crowd became. They were pushing and shoving, demanding that the gate be opened. More soldiers were dispatched to deal with the fire. There was a lot of screaming and shouting. Not just Myriam now, a general air of panic and fear was building. Myriam quickly pushed back through the crowd to where their horses had been secured. Artas and Hendon were already waiting for her there.

"Do you think it's worked?" asked Artas.

"I don't know," replied Myriam. "I haven't seen Ganry yet."

Just then Ganry sprinted back and jumped on his horse.

"Where's Barnaby?" demanded Myriam.

"Follow me, now!" shouted Ganry, pushing his horse Bluebell into the crowd, adding to the confusion and chaos that had broken out in front of the gate, drawing screams, curses, and shouting as Bluebell shouldered past anyone that stood in his way. Myriam, Artas, and Hendon were riding close behind.

As they approached the gate, the remaining soldiers shouted at them to stop. Ganry drew his sword Wind-Storm and without preamble began slashing and swiping at the soldiers seeking to protect the gate. Artas drew his bow and began to assist by picking off any soldiers beyond the reach of Ganry's sword. Myriam could see that Barnaby had been tied to a post not far from the gate, but in the confusion he had been left un-attended, so she spurred her horse Oaken across to him. She jumped down to the ground to cut his ropes, and then helped him clamber up behind her back on to Oaken just as the gates of Athaca swung open and Ganry forced his way through. Ganry paused to make sure that Myriam, Artas and Hendon had all safely made it past the gate, before spurring Bluebell on to canter away from Athaca as quickly as possible.

At the first crossing that they came to, Ganry turned off the road and took one of the trails that led into the Cefinon Forest, finally bringing Bluebell to a halt while they all quickly caught their breath.

"Everyone okay?" asked Ganry, looking over his traveling companions who nodded. "Barnaby?"

"I'm okay, thank you Ganry. I must say that that was the most excitement that I've had in a long time!"

"A dragon?" said Ganry, raising his eyebrow at Myriam. "We're being attacked by a dragon?"

"I was running out of things to say!" protested Myriam. "No one was really panicking enough!"

"Have you ever seen a dragon?" asked Ganry. Myriam shook her head. "Have you ever heard of anyone seeing a dragon?" Myriam shook her head again. "Dragons belong in fairytales for children, but you did well," smiled Ganry. "You all did very well. We got out of there, just. But we need to keep moving and we need to keep moving quickly. We know that they'll come after us as soon as they can and we don't know what else lies ahead. Does anyone know this part of the forest?" They all shook their heads. "Great, then who knows what we'll find. Come on, let's move." Ganry turned Bluebell around and headed off down the forest path, followed by Artas riding Orton, Hendon riding Bartok, and Myriam riding Oaken with Barnaby sitting behind her.

"I've seen a dragon," whispered Barnaby to Myriam.

"Really? Are you just saying that to make me feel better or have you really seen a dragon?"

"Oh they're real," smiled Barnaby mysteriously. "Dragons used to rule these lands but over time their power weakened. Now they live only in the places that are beyond the reach of man. They are shy, but still capable of great things."

"I never know whether to believe you Barnaby, but I do hope that you're right, and that you really did see a dragon. How did you see one if they live only in the places beyond the reach of man?"

"It was purely by accident," explained Barnaby. "I was traveling high in the Basalt mountains when a storm suddenly struck. I quickly looked for shelter and I came across a small cave. I made a fire to try and keep warm and by the light of the fire I could see that the cave continued further into the mountain. I'm quite a curious fellow, so I made myself a torch and explored a bit - it was like a tunnel, leading deeper and deeper into the mountain. I walked along the tunnel, following it down. The further I went the bigger the tunnel became, and after what felt like several miles I suddenly came upon this enormous cavern within the mountain. I couldn't see much, the light from my torch would only shine so far, but as I looked down into the depths of that cavern I could feel the heat, I could smell the acrid smoke of burning, I could see the hot red of fire, I knew that I had entered the lair of a dragon!"

"Is he telling you the dragon story?" asked Hendon, falling back to ride with them.

"Do you believe in dragons Hendon?" asked Myriam.

"If Barnaby says that there are dragons then I believe in dragons."

"Good," said Myriam firmly. "Then I believe in dragons too."

CHAPTER 14

Henrickson pulled his horse to a standstill when they came in sight of the border crossing into Vandemland.

"There it is, Arexos, Vandemland," declared Henrickson. Arexos didn't reply. He still didn't really understand why Henrickson, the captain of the guard at Castle Villerory, Duke Harald's right-hand man, had been sent to Vandemland. As Henrickson's page, Arexos had dutifully followed his master, but he was surprised that they were traveling unaccompanied, and that Henrickson hadn't at least brought a small company of soldiers with him on this mission to the northeastern borders of the Kingdom of Palara. The border crossing looked quiet. There wasn't a great deal of traffic between Palara and Vandemland.

"What are we waiting for sir?" asked Arexos. "Shall we proceed?"

"Have patience Arexos, there's no rush. They're not exactly expecting us."

Arexos looked perplexed. "What do you mean sir? I thought you said that we were here on a trade mission?"

"We are, in a manner of speaking. Duke Harald has asked us to make some inquiries on his behalf while we are here. But it is not an official visit so we don't want to draw too much attention to ourselves. We just need to pass through this border crossing without setting off any alarm bells."

"But sir, you are dressed in the insignia of Castle Villeroy. It's fairly obvious where you are from?" pointed out Arexos.

"I brought a change of clothes with me just for this purpose. It's getting late anyway. There's an inn ahead, we'll spend the night there and then make our crossing into Vandemland in the morning."

Henrickson and Arexos pushed their horses on to the nearby inn, ensuring that their horses had food and water before taking their rucksacks to their room. They found a table in the bar where they could eat their dinner.

"What can I get you gentlemen?" asked the innkeeper, approaching their table. "We have roast venison this evening which is lovely."

"Roast venison sounds good," nodded Henrickson. "And two beers please." The beers arrived quickly and the food not long after.

The innkeeper noted Henrickson's castle guard insignia that he was still wearing. "So what brings you from Castle Villeroy all the way out here?"

"Just part of our normal rounds," reassured Henrickson. "All part of keeping the kingdom safe. Tell me, do you get many people passing through here from Vandemland?"

"Vandemland? No, no one comes from there."

"But the border crossing is just a mile away," insisted Henrickson. "Surely there must be a certain amount of traffic coming and going through there?"

"No, not at all," said the innkeeper, shaking his head. "I can't say with certainty that no one uses the border crossing, but I certainly don't get any customers who have come from Vandemland and are on their way into Palara, and to be fair, I don't get any customers who are heading from here into Vandemland. Why? Are you thinking of going?"

"No no," laughed Henrickson. "Just curious I guess." The innkeep wandered away to let them eat their meal.

"Isn't it going to be difficult for us to pass through the border crossing incognito if they don't actually get any other visitors from Palara?" asked Arexos, wiping up the gravy from his roast venison with a piece of dry bread.

"That is correct. We might need to rethink our approach here. The trouble is that there isn't really any other way across the border - it's such a narrow pass between the cliffs that it effectively forces you through the border crossing that they've built. To avoid it we would have to either travel west through the Berghein Valley and then make an attempt across the Schonbaker Ravine, or we would have to travel further north to the port of Brammanville, and take a boat from there that would land us somewhere along the coast of Vandemland."

Arexos looked forlornly at his finished plate. "They don't guard the coast?"

"Yes, they have look-outs and a patrol, but we would have more chance of evading those along the coast than we would of sneaking through a border crossing." Henrickson pushed his plate away and drank the rest of his beer. "Let's sleep on it for now and we can make a decision in the morning."

The beds in their room at the inn were fairly small and uncomfortable, but Henrickson slept reasonably well. It had been several days of hard riding to get to the border with Vandemland, so it was good to be able to have a night of rest in a proper inn.

Henrickson woke to the smell of coffee.

"I brought you some breakfast," said Arexos, as Henrickson slowly opened his eyes and remembered where they were.

"Well done Arexos, you look after me well."

Arexos began pouring Henrickson a mug of coffee. "I'm not sure that the innkeeper was telling us the whole truth."

"What do you mean?"

"Well I spoke with the stable boy this morning when I went down to check on the horses, and he said that there is some traffic between here and Vandemland."

"Really? Why would the innkeeper lie to us?"

"Well, you were wearing your castle guard insignia last night. You probably scared him. The stable boy says that the traffic between here and Vandemland is done by Narcs. They are gangs of smugglers that operate in this area."

"Smugglers? I hadn't thought of that," pondered Henrickson.

"What would they be smuggling, you think?"

"Jewels, most likely. Jewels and precious metals that come from the mines in Vandemland. They would get a good price for those and there would be plenty of buyers."

"Maybe we could get them to smuggle us in?" suggested Arexos.

"They're hardly going to agree to do that, are they?" laughed Henrickson. "As you've already pointed out, the Narcs aren't going to be particularly welcoming to my castle guard's uniform."

"The stable boy has a contact. I said that you were a mercenary on a spy mission into Vandemland. He said that he would get a message to the Narcs and see if they were willing to transport us across the border."

Henrickson spurted his coffee from his mouth in alarm. "You told a stable boy that I was here on a spy mission!"

"Stable boys don't care about that kind of thing," reassured Arexos. "Neither do Narcs. They just care about money."

"So when do you think we'll hear back from your well-connected stable-boy?"

"Shouldn't take more than a day or two. I said we'd wait here until we heard from him."

"You're quite good at this spying game," smiled Henrickson, admiring the resourcefulness of his young page. "You'd better go get some more coffee. Looks like we're not going anywhere in a hurry."

CHAPTER 15

The mournful sound of a cawing raven somewhere outside the castle walls carried distinctly down into the dungeon of Castle Villeroy.

"Why does he still let us live?" asked King Ludwig, holding his head in his hands in despair.

"Because our daughter continues to elude him," replied Queen Alissia, placing a comforting hand on the arm of her husband.

"She is just a child," sighed King Ludwig. "What hope has she got against Harald and all the armies of the Kingdom?"

"She is not just a child," corrected Queen Alissia with a smile. "Myriam is a resourceful young woman, and she is our daughter. We have taught her well. She was clever enough to avoid capture when Harald took control of the castle, cleverer than we were. I have every faith that she will find a way to stay beyond Harald's reach."

"But why not kill us first while he continues to search for Myriam?" King Ludwig wondered aloud.

"Perhaps I could answer that sire?" It was Lord Holstein, the father of Artas. Loyal supporters of the King, Lord Holstein and his wife Elisabeth had also been imprisoned by Harald. They occupied a cell next to the King and Queen. "If he were to kill you and Queen Alissia now he would still not be able to claim the throne because Princess Myriam would be the rightful heir. He would run the risk of alienating the people of Palara and strengthening support for Myriam. If he can capture Myriam and kill all three of you, then he is next in line to the thrown and he can claim the crown and be free to rule the Kingdom of Palara unopposed."

"Precisely, Lord Holstein," agreed Queen Alissia. "So the safety of our daughter is more important than ever for all of our sakes - and for the future of the kingdom."

"I feel so helpless, locked up here in my own dungeon!" groaned King Ludwig. "I just wish that there was something that I could do to help her!"

"The Queen is right sire," said Lord Holstein quietly. "Princess Myriam is a bright girl, I've no doubt that she is making her way to Castle Locke, to the family of the Queen. She may be there already, preparing an army to march against Harald, to liberate the Kingdom."

"I have a feeling that she hasn't quite made it to safety yet," said the Queen softly. "The roads will all be watched closely, she will have to find another way. I have been dreaming of forests… and fire."

"Fire?" asked King Ludwig. "Why fire? You haven't mentioned fire to me before?"

"I know, I didn't want to worry you. It was just last night, but I dreamed of fire, I dreamed of dragons."

"There's been no news of your son Artas?" asked the King, changing the subject.

"No," replied Lord Holstein. "Again, I think that is a good thing. If he had been captured or killed I think we would know about it by now."

"There is a chance that he is with Myriam," suggested the Queen.

"Really?" Lord Holstein was surprised to hear this. "What makes you say that?"

"My dreams are never very clear," sighed the Queen. "But I do have a strong sense that Myriam is not alone, that she is with friends who are helping to keep her safe. Artas shoots a bow, doesn't he?"

"Why yes. He is a very good archer."

"I feel then that they are together," confirmed the Queen. "I feel that they are both safe."

"Well, that gives me great comfort," said Lord Holstein. "I am proud that he is able to be of service to Princess Myriam."

"How old is your son Artas, now?" asked the King.

"He is now twenty years, sire."

The King cocked his head. "No wife yet?"

"No, afraid not. I have suggested several suitable matches to him but he has declined every one. His passion seems to lie with his archery and his horse. Not that it matters much now I guess."

"If he is able to help Myriam he will help save the kingdom. He will return home a hero and will be able to have his pick of the daughters of all the noble families!" declared the king.

"Perhaps he chooses not to marry?" suggested the Queen. "Like your brother Harald who has never shown the slightest interest in women."

"That damn fool Harald," spat the King furiously. "Betrayed by my own brother!"

CHAPTER 16

"The light is fading, Ganry. How much further do you want to travel?" Artas was a skilled horseman, but riding in the dark with Myriam and Barnaby would not be wise.

"Yes, we should find shelter soon." Ganry looked back from the direction they had come. "This track just seems to be taking us in circles through the forest though."

"We're still heading in a westerly direction." Artas traced the arc of the sun with his hand. "But you're right, this forest does seem to stretch for eternity. Have you not traveled this way before?"

"Normally I stick to the roads," said Ganry with a wry smile. "But the forest does extend all the way to the border of the Kingdom of Palara, so it will at least provide us with cover until then."

"They will come for us in the forest, wont they? They did last time. And now we have Barnaby with us we seem to be moving slower than ever."

"Yes, you're right Artas, but I can't think of any alternative."

"Have you been to the Castle Locke before? Do you know Myriam's grandmother, the Duchess D'Anjue?"

"No, never. I've heard stories of her, but I've never had any business to be in the Berghein Valley. Have you?"

Artas shook his head. "No, but the stories I've heard intrigue me. She seems to be a resourceful woman by all accounts."

"Where are you going with this?"

"What if we could get the Duchess to come to our aid?"

"To send forces across the border, into the Kingdom of Palara? Even if we could get a message to her, I can't imagine she would provoke Duke Harald so blatantly. It would be the perfect excuse for him to launch an attack on Castle Locke, an outright hostile act!"

"Yes, but it is her granddaughter that she would be protecting, and her daughter too. Protecting them from a usurper who has stolen the throne," insisted Artas.

"But would she be strong enough to withstand the might of Palara's armies? To withstand the wrath of Harald?"

"Of that I'm not sure, and I don't think Myriam has much insight into that either. What if I took the message to the Duchess?"

"You?" asked Ganry. "What, ride ahead, while I follow along behind with this motley lot? That leaves me too exposed. I could never protect them if the soldiers caught up with us or if we ran into any trouble."

"Well, what if we sent Hendon?"

"That simple boy has no chance on his own," dismissed Ganry. "He belongs in a cottage in the forest, not riding messages to Castle Locke. No, I think it's best if we stay together and just keep moving as fast as we can. Look, there's a clearing, let's make camp here tonight."

The group quickly got to work and secured the horses and built a fire. Artas went off with his bow to try and find something that could be cooked for dinner.

"I think I can hear a stream close by," announced Hendon. "I'll go and see if there are any fish."

"I'll come with you," said Barnaby, and the two of them bustled off through the trees.

Ganry looked over at Myriam who was tending to the fire. "How are you holding up?"

Myriam appeared pensive. "Do you think we're going to make it to Castle Locke?"

"I can't promise you anything," replied Ganry honestly. "I'm not even exactly sure where we are."

"This forest does seem to be going on for ever." Myriam pulled her cloak around herself as she studied the sturdy old trees that surrounded them on all sides. "If they follow our trail from Athaca it won't take them long to catch up with us, they can't be that far behind."

"I know. Artas and I talked about him riding ahead to ask your grandmother for help, but it seems too risky."

"I know that having Barnaby and Hendon with us slows us down," said Myriam. "But I don't know... there's something about them both that tells me that we're doing the right thing. Hendon is like a woodland spirit, and Barnaby is so old and wise that I can't help thinking that perhaps he could cast a spell or two and keep us all safe."

"Don't let your imagination get away from you," smiled Ganry. "Barnaby is a good storyteller, but that's probably all. Unfortunately I don't think storytelling is going to be much help with keeping us safe from the long arm of Duke Harald."

"I shot a pheasant!" announced Artas proudly, displaying the bird as he came back to the clearing.

"Just one?" asked Ganry. "Looks like it will be a light meal for us all tonight."

"Well it's better than none!" protested Artas, pulling out his knife and beginning to prepare the bird so that it could be roasted over the coals of the fire.

"Thank you for offering to ride ahead, Artas," said Myriam, touching Artas lightly on the shoulder. "It is very brave of you, but I think Ganry's right. I think it's better if we stick together."

Artas continued plucking the feathers of the bird. "When was the last time you saw your grandmother?"

"Not since I was a small child. She came to Castle Villeroy for my twelfth birthday. She told me that my twelfth birthday was an important one, that she had come to give me her blessing. I was scared of her I think, she seemed somehow distant and cold. I hope she remembers me. I hope that she will be willing to help me."

Just then Hendon burst back into the clearing where they had set up camp.

"Quickly!" he gasped. "You have to come and see this!" Ganry, Artas, and Myriam followed Hendon back to where he had left Barnaby. "We came this way looking for a creek or river," explained Hendon. "Barnaby said that he could feel water nearby. We found the creek and followed it down looking for a good spot to fish and then we began hearing this noise, like distant thunder, so we followed it further, and the noise got louder, and then suddenly, we found this!"

"That's amazing!" gasped Myriam in astonishment as they stood at the top of the waterfall, looking down into the churning waters below.

"Look!" pointed Hendon. "There's three different creeks, all feeding into these falls, from here it seems to form a fairly substantial river."

"What river would that be then?" asked Artas.

"I've no idea!" admitted Myriam.

"It would have been helpful if your tutor had focused a bit more on geography lessons instead of romantic poetry," said Ganry sarcastically.

"Which direction is the river flowing?" Artas crouched down to get close to the water. "Do you think it's heading west? Maybe we could follow it as a way through the forest?"

"It's getting too dark now to do anything about it anyway." Ganry turned to walk back to their camp. "Catch some fish Hendon and let's get some food in our bellies. We can think about how we tackle it in the morning."

They had agreed to take it in turns to keep watch during the night. Myriam took first watch, handing over to Hendon, who woke Ganry when it was his turn.

"Everything okay?" asked Ganry quietly as Hendon roused him from his sleep.

Hendon yawned. "The forest is watching over us. See, there is an owl in the tree above us, and those eyes over near the tree belong to a fox."

"Do you really talk with animals?"

"I don't know," replied Hendon. "Sometimes I think that I can hear what they're thinking, sometimes I can't. Barnaby is better at it than I am. He can have whole conversations just by looking in the eyes of an animal. He always says that goats are very intelligent, but I think foxes and owls are cleverer than goats."

Ganry added a log of wood to the fire and propped himself up against one of the nearby trees. "Get some sleep kid. I'll keep the fox and the owl company for a while."

Ganry stared out into the deep darkness of the surrounding forest. He almost found it amusing that the strange twists and turns of his life had brought him to this point, sitting in the middle of an unfamiliar forest, on the run from everyone, trying to keep a disparate group of travelers safe from harm. He was a long way away from the plains of Mirnee - not just geographically, but in every sense of the word. He wondered whether the Emperor Fontleroy was still ruling, now known as Fontleroy the Mad. It had been a while since Ganry had had any news from Mirnee, there wasn't really anything connecting him to that place now. He had left with nothing but his horse, Bluebell, and his sword, WindStorm.

WindStorm lay across his knees, secured safely in it's scabbard. He always liked to keep it close. It gave him a sense of security, one of the few constants in his life since he had lost his wife and daughter. The truth was that he didn't really know much about the origins of WindStorm. It had belonged to his father, a big man with a big imagination. Ganry's father had been a proud warrior and WindStorm had been his most prized possession. He had always told Ganry that WindStorm was forged in the fires of the Grimlock blade-smiths who lived in the Limestone Mountains, but Ganry had no way of knowing if this was true. Ganry had idolized his father, like a god. As a child Ganry had helped polish his father's armor, helping him to prepare for battle. Before leaving the house to head off to war, Ganry's father would take his sword from his scabbard and hold it high above his head, shouting at the top of his voice:

"I am Davide de Rosenthorn! I wield the mighty WindStorm! I yield to no man!" He said that this is what he shouted as he attacked his enemies, as they fell beneath his sword. It was the battle cry that Ganry had also adopted, just as he had also adopted his father's sword.

Ganry chuckled to himself as he silently mouthed the words. He knew that one day he would meet the man who would prove him wrong. When you live life as a mercenary you knew that it was only a matter of time before your life ended violently. He knew that he would die one day, but he hoped that he would be able to survive a little longer, perhaps long enough to deliver Myriam to her grandmother at Castle Locke. It was a small thing, and it probably didn't mean much in the grand scheme of the world, but he felt that if he could just do this one good deed then his life may have had some meaning, some purpose.

Ganry missed his father. He missed those days of long ago when his father was a god, when his father was invincible. His father hadn't died a hero's death. He hadn't died on the battlefield with his sword held high. He had been poisoned, dying a wretched, painful death in his bed. Ganry blamed his step-mother but none of his uncles would believe him. So Ganry took hold of WindStorm and left the family home to join the armies of the Emperor Fontleroy. He looked at the sword that lay across his knees. A sword that had drawn a lot of blood, a sword that had taken many lives. A sword that was the only connection that he had to the father that he admired so much.

CHAPTER 17

"So what do you think?" said Artas, staring down at the churning waters at the bottom of the waterfall. "There doesn't seem to be any trail running along beside the river, it's just cutting straight through the trees."

"We should build a raft!" declared Hendon excitedly.

"A raft?" said Ganry in disbelief. "You want to float down the river?"

"Yes! That would be perfect! We could float down the river on a raft!"

"But what would we do with the horses?"

"They could swim behind the raft!"

"They can't swim long distances, they get tired quickly."

"Well, we could take lots of breaks as we go," insisted Hendon.

"It would get us off the trail and make our tracks impossible to follow," added Myriam.

"What if there's more waterfalls downstream?" protested Ganry. "A raft isn't much good to us if it floats us over the edge of a giant waterfall."

"We'll be taking it slowly with the horses anyway," suggested Artas. "So we can always have one of us scouting ahead."

"And who's going to build the raft?" Ganry was not convinced. "Do any of you know how to build a raft that will take the weight of all five of us?"

"Actually, I have a lot of experience with raft building," interjected Barnaby quietly.

"Barnaby, you are full of surprises!" laughed Myriam. "Well I think that settles it! If we stay on that forest trail it is inevitable that Duke Harald's men will catch us and either kill us instantly or drag us back in chains. Trying to raft our way through the forest on this river is by no means a perfect solution, but it at least gives us some hope of trying to stay a step ahead of our pursuers. Don't you agree Ganry?"

"I guess you're right," grumbled Ganry.

"Right," said Myriam, taking charge. "Hendon and Barnaby, you see if you can find a safe path for us that will get us down to the bottom of the falls. We'll gather up the horses and our gear and then we'll be ready to make a start."

It was a slow descent, carefully leading the horses down the steep bank that took them to the level of the river at the base of the falls. Barnaby quickly set to work and began constructing the raft, finding suitable logs and binding them expertly together with ropes and vines. In no time the raft was ready to go.

"I have to admit Barnaby, that is a particularly solid looking raft," admired Ganry.

"Well let's just take it fairly slowly to begin with," cautioned Barnaby. "It's quite a heavy load that we're carrying and we're not really sure how fast this river is flowing."

"I'll swim with the horses," offered Hendon. "Just to get them settled at the start."

"Okay, let's load up and slowly push off," said Ganry, not feeling as certain or confident as he was trying to sound. They used long poles to maneuver the raft away from the bank and out into the current of the river. The horses were tied to the back of the logs and Hendon led them into the water. He began swimming alongside them as they became used to this new method of transport.

Ganry peered at the slow moving current. "No snakes in this river is there?"

"You're obsessed with snakes!" laughed Artas. "I'm pretty sure that there are no snakes in this river."

"Pretty sure?" Ganry raised an eyebrow. "It's just that in the marshes of Llandaff there were water snakes that were pretty vicious."

"How big were the marsh snakes?" asked Myriam.

"The biggest that I ever saw was ten feet long, but there were stories of real monsters that could sink a small boat," replied Ganry, looking carefully once more at the river water.

"Ten feet is big enough, thanks!" gasped Myriam.

"Are they poisonous?" Artas was curious.

"I don't think so." Ganry dragged his hand in the water to see if he could catch any movement underneath. "They're constrictors, they wrap around your body until you can't breathe anymore."

"No wonder you didn't go swimming in the marches," shivered Myriam. "I've never heard of any snakes like that in the rivers of Palara, but then again I didn't really know that this river existed, so I guess anything is possible."

"Well if one of the horses suddenly goes missing, I'm getting off the raft," said Ganry firmly.

The river flowed smoothly and the raft made good progress, floating along through the thick forest of trees that lined both banks.

"We'd better take a break soon!" said Hendon, pulling himself up on to the raft. "The horses are starting to tire."

"Okay, there's a sandbank on that next bend in the river, let's aim for that." Ganry took hold of one of their steering poles and began to guide the raft in the direction of the sandbank. The horses seemed relieved to have their hooves back on solid ground, but they sensed that it was only a momentary respite from the river, so quickly began to graze on the grasses that grew along the banks.

"You're a genius, Hendon!" congratulated Myriam. "This raft is working out so well!"

"Well, Barnaby is the raft builder. That's the real skill," Hendon smiled modestly, clearly pleased with the praise from the Princess.

"You know, I'm losing all track of distance and direction," said Artas, looking up into the sky. "It's hard to see much beyond the canopy of the forest, and the way that the river twists and turns, I'm not even totally sure which direction we're heading in anymore."

"So you're saying that we could be just floating around in circles?" asked Ganry.

"Well, not exactly," laughed Artas. "The river has to be flowing somewhere. I'm just not totally sure that it's taking us where we want to go. Barnaby, any ideas?"

"The Cefinon Forest holds many secrets and surprises," replied Barnaby sagely.

"Well we don't have many options really," acknowledged Ganry. "We're just going to have to keep floating along and see where the river decides to take us."

CHAPTER 18

"Sir, I think you should come down to the stables with me now," said Arexos, opening the door to the room that he was sharing with Henrickson, at the inn near the border crossing with Vandemland.

"What is it, Arexos?"

"The stable boy has a message from the Narcs."

"The smugglers? Right, let's go." Henrickson followed Arexos down the stairs and out into the back yard of the inn.

"Psst!" hissed the stable boy, seeing them approach. "Go down the back, the end stall."

Arexos led the way and Henrickson followed cautiously, his hand resting lightly on the hilt of the dagger that he had tucked into his belt. Waiting for them in the last stall was a shady looking man, a member of the gang of Narcs that smuggled anything of value in to and out of Vandemland.

"So you want to get into Vandemland?" asked the Narc.

"Yes, is that possible?" Henrickson watched him carefully.

"Anything is possible. For a price."

"How soon could you get us across the border?"

"Our next run is tomorrow night."

"How do you get past the border crossing?"

"Now if I told you that I would be giving away all of our secrets," smirked the Narc. "You don't need to worry about that. You'll be blind-folded. We'll take the blindfolds off once you're safely on the other side."

"Blindfolded! Is that really necessary?" protested Henrickson.

"Like I said, we can't give away all of our secrets," repeated the Narc.

"What about getting back across the border? How would we contact you to arrange that?"

"My boss will give you a time and place where we'll collect you for the return journey. If you miss that pick-up then you're on your own. Any other questions?"

"No. I think that's all I need to know for now."

"Right, we'll pick you up here tomorrow night at sundown. Make sure you have your money ready," hissed the Narc as he disappeared into the night.

"I'm not convinced that this is a good idea," said Henrickson to Arexos as they made their way back up the stairs to their room. "But I don't think we've got too many other options at this stage."

"Are you sure that we need to go into Vandemland, sir? Couldn't you just go back to Duke Harald and explain that the border crossing was closed?"

"While that does sound fairly tempting Arexos, I'm afraid that we don't have that luxury. Duke Harald would see that as a failure and he really doesn't tolerate failure."

The next evening, just after sunset, Henrickson and Arexos were sitting in their room at the inn when they heard a long, low whistle from down in the yard.

"I'm guessing that that's our signal," said Henrickson, and they gathered up their rucksacks and headed down to the stables.

"Good evening gentlemen," greeted the Narc that they had met with the previous night. "Money first please." Henrickson handed over the price that had been agreed. With payment completed, Henrickson and Arexos were instructed to mount their horses and then a black bag was placed over each of their heads.

From that point their journey into Vandemland was a mystery to Henrickson. They seemed to be surrounded by men on horses as they were led along. There wasn't a lot of talking, but he heard different accents that he couldn't place. The bag over his head completely disoriented him and he lost track of how long they had been riding for, and he had no clue as to which direction they were riding in. Eventually their horses came to a stop and he was roughly helped to dismount from his horse before the bag was removed from his head.

"Where are we?" Henrickson quickly looked around and tried to get his bearings.

"This is the slave market of eastern Vandemland," sneered the Narc.

"But why have you brought us here?" asked Henrickson, confused.

"Because we have just sold you to the highest bidder, slave!" laughed the Narc, quickly securing Henrickson's hands and feet with chains.

"You can't do that! I am the captain of the palace guard!" protested Henrickson.

"Different country, different rules," grinned the Narc. "The soldiers of the Kingdom of Palara have been a pain in our neck for too long. It's about time we got some sort of compensation. I told your new owner that you thrive on hard work, but that if you give him any trouble then the only discipline that you understand is the whip. I think you're going to like it here."

"Wait, where's Arexos? What have you done with my page?" shouted Henrickson.

"He's not your page anymore, is he?" laughed the Narc. "We sold him as a body slave to one of the rich nobles. He'll be feeding grapes to a fat old man before the sun comes up."

Henrickson looked desperately around him. He could see immediately that there was no chance of escape. Not only was he bound by chains, but the Narcs were well armed and clearly pleased with the profit that they had made on the sale.

The slave market was a busy, bustling place - full of men of all shapes and sizes, exotic looking men of a type that he hadn't seen before. He guessed that they came from somewhere across the Damatine Sea. A large, fierce looking man approached Henrickson and grabbed him by the chains that bound him, dragging him across to a flat-bed wagon on which a few other dejected looking men were sitting. They were also in chains. Once Henrickson was loaded onto the wagon, it lurched off down a rough track and Henrickson was helpless to do anything but curse his own foolishness for being so easily tricked into this disastrous situation.

CHAPTER 19

"What do you mean she escaped!" roared Duke Harald, infuriated by the news that the messenger had brought to him. "She is a fifteen year old girl! How in the gods' name did she manage to escape from a town where the gates were locked and the soldiers of Palara stood guard!" The messenger knew that this was probably a rhetorical question, so he knelt silently in front of the Duke, keeping still, while the Duke's rage echoed around the room. "Where is Henrickson?" shouted Harald. There was no answer. There was no one else in the throne room apart from the quivering messenger who had his eyes averted and was concentrating on a chipped stone in the floor. Harald suddenly grabbed the messenger by the hair and pulled his head back, forcing him to look him in the face. "I asked you a question!" spat Harald menacingly. "Where is Henrickson?"

"Sir, there's been no word from him. Not since you sent him to Vandemland," stuttered the messenger.

"Get out!" shouted Harald, spitting a mouthful of saliva into the face of the young messenger. "Get out! Get out! Get out!" The messenger hastily exited the room, relieved to have escaped with his head still attached to his shoulders.

Harald slumped dejectedly onto the throne. It was a beautiful piece of furniture. Solid, dependable. It had been the throne of the Kingdom of Palara for centuries, long before Duke Harald's family had come to power. The throne was a relatively simple design, made from oak that had been felled from the Cefinon Forest. It was inlaid with gold and precious stones, creating the image of an eagle in the tall back rest, so when you sat on the throne, the majestic bird of prey hovered above you. Studying it, Duke Harald wondered why an eagle had been chosen as the symbol of the Kingdom of Palara. In all his years of hunting he had had never seen an eagle in these lands.

In keeping with the throne itself, the rest of the room was not lavish but it had a sense of grandeur, a sense of occasion. There was a plain chair to the left of the throne. This is where the Queen would sit. The stone was of slate. It wasn't an enormous room - just large enough for the King to receive important visitors, delegations from neighboring kingdoms, or trade partners. This is where official declarations are made and where commandments are issued. It is from this room that the Kingdom of Palara is governed.

The walls were decorated with tapestries - detailed pieces that told the history of the Kingdom and the history of Duke Harald's family. Harald remembered studying these tapestries as a child. He and his brother had an old eccentric tutor who had sought permission to bring them into the throne room so that they could learn their history. They were taught the journey, the circumstances, the events that had brought the Kingdom of Palara into existence, and the triumph that had been the ascension of Duke Harald's family to the throne.

As he sat, dejected, staring at the walls, he tried to recall those stories now. How the displaced tribes came down from the Basalt Mountains and claimed the forests as the floods receded, how the great chief Terrick had united the tribes, imposing control brutally and without mercy, bringing the people together and founding the Kingdom of Palara.

Palara was an ancient word that meant "The beauty is in the skies". After a seemingly endless period of rain that had submerged all of the low lying land, the sun finally broke through and blue skies reappeared. Terrick declared that they would never forget the beauty of a clear blue sky. That was a long time ago, and much had changed since the days of the great chief Terrick.

The Castle Villeroy had been built by Duke Harald's great-grandfather, the grandfather of his father. His name was Lord Ironbark, or at least that's what everyone referred to him as. He claimed the throne of Palara by killing everyone that stood in his way - a tactic that had always impressed the young, studious Harald. Before Ironbark had come to power, the kings of Palara had lived in long, wooden houses, but Ironbark felt that a king needed to have a seat of power that reflected his worth. He brought in stonemasons and master builders from the east to build a castle that could not only be defended against the most ferocious attack, but a castle that sent a signal to the world that this was the home of a king, this was the home of the King of Palara.

In the history of the Kingdom there had never been a Queen that had taken the throne. There was nothing in the laws of the kingdom that forbade it, but it was clear that sons took precedence over daughters and throughout the history of the kingdom, there had always been a son born who had been the rightful heir. As the only child of Ludwig, Princess Myriam was set to be the first Queen to rule the Kingdom of Palara. That was one of the reasons that had emboldened Harald to take control. There was a lot of disquiet amongst the noble families about having a woman rule them. As soon as he could capture Myriam, he would put this nonsense to an end and claim the throne as the only and rightful heir.

CHAPTER 20

"Well done Artas. That's a good fire," complimented Ganry, as Artas prepared a bed of fiery coal over which they could cook some food.

"Look at these beauties!" exclaimed Hendon, returning from the river where he had quickly caught enough silvery trout to feed them all.

"The horses are munching happily away!" announced Myriam, having safely secured the horses nearby. "They seemed pretty happy to be on solid ground. I didn't have the heart to tell them it was only a temporary respite from their swimming."

Ganry sat down on a log near the fire. He was proud of his brave little crew of travelers. Against all odds they were still safe, still moving along on their journey.

"What do you think, Barnaby?" Ganry asked as the older man took a seat beside him on the sandbank where they had made camp. "Should we stay here for the night or should we push on and try and get a bit further down river?"

"Well, that depends…"

"Depends on what?"

"Whether you are still trying to reach Castle Locke."

"Are you saying that in order to reach Castle Locke, we need to get back on the raft and keep moving along the river?"

"This river doesn't take us to Castle Locke. This river doesn't flow to the Berghein Valley," said Barnaby.

"I thought you didn't know this part of the forest? How do you know that this river won't take us to the Berghein Valley?" demanded Ganry.

"The fish told me."

"Great! Now we're taking directions from fish!" exclaimed Ganry. "I prefer to eat fish, not take directions from them. Are they cooked yet, Hendon?"

"Where do you think this river leads Barnaby?" asked Myriam quietly.

"It doesn't leave the forest."

"But it has to flow somewhere, doesn't it?" asked Artas.

"It does," agreed Barnaby. "But it doesn't leave the forest."

"Well, whether that's the case or not, it is the only way we've got to travel at the moment, so my view is that we have to keep following this river to wherever it is taking us," said Ganry firmly.

"But what if it isn't taking us West?" Myriam was concerned. "What if it is taking us further away from Castle Locke?"

"I think that's a risk that we'll need to take. We're so deep in this forest now that it is too late to try and turn around and find a road. Let's camp here for the night. It's a good sandbar, we've got a fire going, and it will give the horses a chance to rest. We can continue on our raft down the river tomorrow and see where it takes us."

Night soon fell and the travelers all found a place to sleep near the fire. Ganry took first watch, throwing a log on the fire to keep the coals glowing.

"Can't sleep?" asked Ganry, as Artas came to sit beside him.

"No. I'm worried about my family. I set out to try and find a way to rescue them from the dungeons of Castle Villeroy, but now we just seem to be getting further and further away, and now we're not even sure where we are."

"I know kid, I know. Things haven't really turned out as we'd hoped. But right now I don't think we've got too many options."

"I understand. I just feel a bit helpless, that's all. We seem to have been traveling for a long time but we're really not sure if we're any closer to where we're trying to get to."

They sat in a comfortable silence, watching the flames dance, creating flickering shadows around them.

Ganry watched as Artas fiddled with his bow. "Why did you take up archery? Most boys from noble families are taught to use a sword."

"I was always pretty small for my age," Artas said, now checking the fletching on his arrows. "I was never very strong. The other boys always beat me at wrestling. When it came to learning to wield a sword I really wasn't strong enough to lift a full-sized one, let alone be able to fend off an opponent with it. So my tutor suggested that instead of trying to compete with the stronger boys that I try a different tactic, so he taught me archery."

"You've done pretty well at it."

"Thanks," chuckled Artas. "It made me look at things a bit differently, it made me feel strong and powerful which was something that I'd never felt before. To realize that I didn't need to be tall or muscular in order to win a fight. I guess you wouldn't understand that."

"I wasn't always this size. I'm a lot older than you, remember."

"And who taught you how to use a sword?"

Ganry hesitated for a beat. "My father."

"Is he still alive?"

"No, he died," said Ganry, stirring the coals of the fire.

"In battle?"

"Surprisingly not. He was a warrior but he was poisoned by my step-mother. I guess that you could say that he was killed in the battle of love."

"I don't have a lot of experience in that department," said Artas, bashfully.

"You're only young kid, plenty of time for that. I wouldn't worry about it." Ganry put his arm in a brotherly way around Artas's shoulders and punched him lightly.

Artas shrugged him off with a laugh. "Have you ever been married?"

"Yes, I had a wife and a daughter, they're both dead now," replied Ganry darkly.

"I'm sorry, I didn't mean to pry," apologised Artas.

"It's okay, it seems a long time ago now. A different time, a different place, a different life."

The silence around them lengthened. Artas looked over at Myriam, sleeping peacefully. Her blond hair was untied and lay around her face like rays of the sun. "Why are you protecting Myriam?"

"What do you mean?" Ganry raised an eyebrow. "I'm a mercenary, she is paying me to protect her."

"There's more to it than that," pushed Artas. "No gold is worth the danger that you have placed yourself in on this journey. Whatever she is paying you, you could get double that from Duke Harald if you delivered her to him, I'm sure."

"Hmm, I guess you're right. I never thought about that. I could always use more gold." Ganry chuckled lightly at the shocked expression on Artas's face. "Just kidding. You know, I'm really not sure. It just seems to be the right thing to do. A chance to do something good for once. A chance to be a hero." He poked at the fire, causing the flames to dance higher.

CHAPTER 21

"Let's go slaves!" The whip cracked as the wagon pulled to a stop and Henrickson and the other men were pulled down on to the ground.

Betrayed by the Narcs, the smugglers, Henrickson had been sold into slavery in Vandemland. He looked around the desolate landscape. They had arrived at some kind of mine. The dust and the heat were almost unbearable. Henrickson had heard about the mines of Vandemland, but this was beyond anything that he had ever imagined - a vast pit, a deep scar on the land. Henrickson could see thousands of men at work, down in the depths of the mine, hauling loads of rubble up small, narrow ladders, with vicious looking overseers cracking their whips to keep the men working.

The secretive kingdom of Vandemland was known for producing some of the world's most precious stones and gems, and now Henrickson could see how they did it. Duke Harald had sent Henrickson, the captain of his guard, to scope out Vandemland, to gather information, to prepare for an attack. This wasn't quite what he had planned.

"Get to work slaves!" growled one of the foremen, thrusting a pick towards Henrickson. Henrickson reluctantly took hold of the tool and followed the overseer through the clouds of dust and down towards the ladders that would take them into the depths of the mine. "You dig the rock and carry it to the surface. Simple," explained the overseer.

The slaves working on the mine seemed to be from all sorts of different countries, all different sizes, shapes, colors, and languages. All of them with one thing in common: they were all slaves of Vandemland.

The overseers looked liked grizzled old warriors, wearing leather chest-plates and armed with short, straight daggers. The whips that they wielded though were their most threatening weapon. They didn't hesitate to bring the stinging strip of leather down across the back of any slave that they felt wasn't working hard enough, wasn't working quick enough, or wasn't being obedient enough.

The rock that they were digging into was relatively soft, crumbling beneath the pick as Henrickson swung it, slamming the iron spike into the cliff face. The bucket once filled had to be carried all the way back up to the top of the mine. Henrickson wasn't sure what they were even looking for. It was a combination of sandy soil and hard lumps of rock that he was loading into his bucket. He had been told to just take it all to the top.

The unfamiliar motion of the pick soon blistered the skin on his hands, making each digging movement painful. Henrickson knew that he had to find a way to escape from the mine, escape from the captivity of Vandemland. So far he hadn't really learned anything that might help Duke Harald's plan to invade the country, but it was clear that there was great wealth buried beneath the soil of these dry, arid mountains.

"Dig faster!" growled an overseer standing behind Henrickson, and he soon felt the sharp stinging pain of the whip biting into his skin across his back, the force of the blow knocking him to the ground.

"Come on, keep up," said one of the slaves next to him, helping him back to his feet. "Don't give them a reason to hurt you."

"You speak my language? Are you from Palara?" asked Henrickson, quickly getting to his feet and collecting his pick so that he could continue working.

"Once I was..." replied the man. "But I doubt I will ever see my home again. I am Ragnald."

"I am Henrickson. How long have you been here?"

"Several weeks now. They captured the ship that I was on, just off the coast here."

"You're a sailor?"

"A merchant. I was heading for the port of Brammanville. We must have strayed into waters that belonged to Vandemland. We were surrounded by their ships and boarded. They took everyone prisoner. Anyone that resisted was killed."

"What are our chances of escape?" Henrickson tried to talk discreetly while continuing to chip away at the rock in front of him, loading his bucket and preparing to lug it up the ladders to the top of the mine.

"Of course I've thought about escape," hissed Ragnald. "Everyone thinks of escape, but there is no way to escape. Where would you go? It is a day's journey to the coast but they are just sheer cliffs down on to the rocks below. In the other direction is the Schonbaker Ravine which is totally impassable, and then everywhere else is desert. There's not just the overseers to think about, there are guards surrounding the perimeter of the mine. Every day they execute the men that have tried to escape. They don't just execute them, they draw and quarter them, tearing them apart while their screams echo around the mine."

"That does sound a bit of a challenge." Henrickson remained undeterred. "But we've got to find a way out of here. I'm not ending my days in this hell-hole of a mine. I'd prefer to try and escape and be executed like a warrior than die at the end of a whip like a miserable slave. Will you come with me?"

"You're a fool," said Ragnald, shaking his head. "You have no chance of escaping. I would prefer to take my chances here."

"Then you are a coward," spat Henrickson. "You deserve to die a slave. I will fight for my freedom."

CHAPTER 22

"What news, Zander?" demanded Duchess D'Anjue impatiently as her chief counsel entered her throne room.

"Duchess," greeted Zander, bending down on one knee on the stone floor and bowing deeply in a formal greeting.

"Enough with the bowing, Zander!" dismissed the Duchess impatiently. "What news have our messengers brought from the Kingdom of Palara?"

"It is not good news I'm afraid, Duchess," began Zander. "Our agents have confirmed that Duke Harald has seized control."

"But what of King Ludwig and my daughter Alissia? What has become of them?" demanded the Duchess urgently.

"Their fate remains unclear. They were certainly taken prisoner but that is all the information we have at the moment."

"Has Duke Harald claimed the throne? Has he declared himself king?"

"No, it does not appear so."

"That means that they're still alive!" said the Duchess, thumping the arm of her wooden throne. "He can't claim the throne while the rightful king is still alive. Tell me Zander, what news of my granddaughter, Myriam, was she also taken prisoner?"

"We weren't able to find out anything concrete regarding Myriam I'm afraid," replied Zander somberly. "There were some reports that she had been taken prisoner, but then also some rumors that she had in fact escaped."

"I wonder..." said the Duchess to herself, thoughtfully, looking into the distance. "It's strange that we've had no word from Myriam's tutor, Leonidavus. I wonder if they have perhaps managed to escape? I have had dreams about her recently... vivid dreams... that would make sense, that she is calling for me, searching for me, needing my assistance. If only we knew where she was, but all I see in my dreams is water..."

Leonidavus had been one of the Duchess's most trusted advisors. She had sent him to tutor her granddaughter Myriam so that she would know her history, that she would understand her family and their eternal rule of Castle Locke at the top of the Berghein Valley.

The Duchess had been pleased with the match of her daughter Alissia to the future king of Palara. She had never thought that Ludwig was particularly bright or inspiring, but he was solid and dependable, and he was the heir to the throne. The Duchess didn't know much about the brother, Duke Harald. She had met him only once or twice. It was in Leonidavus's last report to her that he had first mentioned his concerns that Duke Harald had designs on the throne of Palara. The Duchess was angry with herself for not taking that warning more seriously, for not having taken action sooner to ensure the protection of her family.

"Duchess..." said Zander tentatively, cautious about interrupting the Duchess's train of thought.

"Yes Zander, what is it?"

"Would you like me to take a small detachment of men and go into the Kingdom of Palara to search for Myriam?"

"That is tempting. But where would you look? My dreams aren't particularly clear. I can't give you a map reference. Besides, I'm cautious about antagonizing Harald too much. If I sent an armed party across the border he could easily claim it as an act of aggression, giving him an excuse to crush us with his vastly superior army."

"We could disguise ourselves?" suggested Zander. "If we weren't wearing the colors of Locke then we could pass for mercenaries or traders just riding through."

"But would you even recognize Myriam? How would you know who you were looking for?"

"I have served your family all my life. I believe will recognize her. My men are skilled hunters. If she is still alive we will find her."

"She will be scared and unsure who she can trust," replied the Duchess, clearly warming to the idea. "She wears the ring of Locke, the matching one to mine." The Duchess held up her left hand to display the glowing ring. "Take my dagger with you, it carries the same stones. She will know it as being of this place. The stones glow brighter when they are brought together." Zander held out both hands and carefully received the small precious dagger from the Duchess. "How many men will you take with you?"

"Just four plus myself. The main road is heavily guarded by the soldiers of Palara. We will need to find an alternate path in order to try and avoid their attention."

"Then you will have to enter the forest. Do you know the forest of Cefinon?"

"Does anyone know the forest of Cefinon?" said Zander with a smile.

"You're right. That vast ancient forest remains a mystery to us all. But if the road is heavily guarded then there is no other way to travel between here and Palara, which means that if Myriam is trying to reach me then she must also be trying to travel through the forest. When can you leave?"

"I will leave immediately, Duchess. My men can be ready within the hour."

"Excellent. Go!" instructed the Duchess. "Look for water, Zander. My dreams show me only water."

The Duchess stood from her throne and walked across to one of the windows that looked out across the Berghein Valley. This protected valley with its rich farmlands had been the home of her family for generations. This castle had remained strong and powerful while the lands beyond its borders had frequently torn themselves apart as various factions vied for power and control. The Duchess wondered whether she had the strength to once again withstand the storm that was brewing beyond the walls of her home. The storm, which had already engulfed her precious daughter, was now threatening her even more precious granddaughter.

CHAPTER 23

"The river seems to be slowing down." Hendon was keenly observing the current as their raft floated along, trailing the four horses who gamely swum along behind them.

"You're right," nodded Barnaby.

"We're coming in to that bend up ahead," pointed out Artas. "It could be a place to stop and let the horses rest."

"I can't see any sign of a sand-bank though," countered Ganry. "It's almost as if those trees are growing out of the water."

"Let's sit tight for a bit longer," suggested Myriam. "There might be a sandbank around the corner that we can pull into."

The five travelers clung to their sturdy raft as it followed the flow of the river around the bend. As they slowly swung around, they found themselves confronted by a flotilla of small fishing boats and a forest of spears pointed in their direction.

"It looks like they were expecting us," observed Ganry wryly.

The fishermen quickly secured ropes to the raft and began to drag it along behind them. As they moved forward, the party-of-five began to understand why the river had been slowing down. They had entered a massive lake concealed completely within the forest.

"Lake men," said Barnaby with growing concern.

"What does that mean?" growled Ganry impatiently. "Who are these *lake men*?"

"I've heard of them before, but never knew how to find them. They have very little contact with the outside world."

"They don't seem very friendly." Artas looked warily around.

"They're probably just scared."

"So am I," shivered Myriam.

The fishermen towed the raft into their settlement. To Ganry's eyes it was a strange, ramshackle collection of wooden houses built on stilts over the water. Once the raft was secured against one of the walkways, the five passengers were instructed to disembark.

"The horses?" Ganry gestured towards the four horses that had been towed along behind the raft. Several of the fishermen quickly worked to untie the horses and led them along to a lower walkway where they could be pulled out of the water.

"Who are you?" demanded a tall, imposing man who emerged from one of the houses. He had an air of importance. The other lake men clearly deferred to him. Ganry assumed him to be the tribe's leader.

"We are holiday-makers, heading west."

"No one travels on this river," replied the lake man. "No one travels on a raft like yours. We have been following you since you entered our territory. You are lucky that the water dragons didn't eat you."

"Water dragons?" *They sound worse than snakes,* thought Ganry.

"I asked who you are!" shouted the lake man. "Answer me now or I will have you all killed!"

"I am Princess Myriam from Castle Villeroy, the heir to the Kingdom of Palara," said Myriam respectfully, stepping forward to try and defuse the situation. The lake man studied her carefully.

"The Kingdom of Palara means nothing to us here," said the lake man darkly. "We are beyond your control."

"I acknowledge your independence," replied Myriam.

"Why would a Princess of Palara be floating along the hidden river on a raft?"

"We are in danger. My family has been taken prisoner. We need to get to the west to safety."

"You're going the wrong way."

"What do you mean, going the wrong way?" demanded Ganry.

"I am not here to answer your questions," spat the lake man, clearly unimpressed by Ganry's tone. "You are my prisoners. No one enters the lake without my permission and you do not have my permission! Lock them up!" He gestured to his men to take Ganry and the others away. "Leave the girl with me."

"No!" shouted Ganry, struggling against the men that had him firmly tied with rope.

Myriam shivered with fear as the lake man led her back inside his wooden hut. She saw that it was small and damp. There was little sign of comfort or warmth. She could hear the water of the lake washing beneath the floor of the hut. She had to admit she was scared of what his intentions might be.

"You have no need to fear me," said the lake man, sensing Myriam's apprehension. "Please, take a seat. Are you hungry? Thirsty?" Myriam nodded as she sat on a cushion on the wooden floor. "You can see that you have created a problem for us. This is one of our main fishing villages. The secrecy of this lake is the only thing that has kept us strong and independent all of these years, and then suddenly you appear - the heir to the throne of Palara."

"We don't want any trouble." Myriam felt calmer now that the man was displaying some form of civility. Her natural curiosity kicked in. "You have other villages? How many of you are there?"

"There are several thousand of us. Our main settlement is on the other side of the lake, hidden within the trees."

"And you are their leader?"

"I am Clay, the chief of the lake men." He smiled broadly, revealing a full set of yellowed teeth.

"Sir, please..." began Myriam, thinking about her own quest. "My companions and I need your help. We are in great danger. We must get to Castle Locke."

"The home of Duchess D'Anjue?"

"She is my grandmother. Do you know her?"

"I owe no allegiance to Castle Locke, but then again I owe no allegiance to Castle Villeroy," replied Clay.

"My ancestors fought hard to survive the great floods. When the tribes descended from the Basalt Mountains, my ancestors struggled to retain their territory, and to protect the forest. Since that time our continued existence has depended on secrecy, and on being hidden. Every fiber in my being screams at me to kill you and your companions immediately. Your very presence here is a threat to everything that we have fought so hard to build."

Myriam involuntarily jerked back from the menace in his eyes. "Please sir! Please spare us!" begged Myriam. "I promise that we won't betray you!"

"Well," pondered Clay, looking her up and down with a half-smile and licking his thin lips. "I may have a proposition for you…"

CHAPTER 24

"My brother is a traitor to the Kingdom of Palara and is to be executed!" declared Duke Harald, slamming his fist down on the table, causing the old judge to jump in alarm. They met in the throne room but Duke Harald did not sit on the throne. He knew to sit there would not be proper until he had been duly declared King of the realm. The old man sitting across from him was Judge Strogen, the Chief Judge of Palara. It was Judge Strogen that needed to sign the order that would confirm Duke Harald as the rightful claimant to the throne; the order that was needed before Duke Harald could be crowned as the rightful King of Palara.

"Will there be a trial of your brother's crimes?" asked the judge tentatively, nervously smoothing his robes as he did his best to avoid Harald's steely gaze.

"There is no need for a trial," dismissed Harald. "The evidence is irrefutable."

"And when will the execution take place?" asked the judge.

"Within seven days," replied the Harald bluntly.

"And the family of King Ludwig? What will be their fate?"

"Queen Alissia will also be executed. She is complicit in her husband's guilt," spat Harald.

"So that will leave Princess Myriam as the heir to the throne?"

"No… it will not!" growled Duke Harald fiercely. "Myriam will be executed also. The guilt of her father stains the whole family."

"My understanding was that you do not currently have Myriam in custody?" asked Judge Strogen, feeling the anger emanating from the Duke across the table.

"That is irrelevant!" shouted Harald, becoming increasingly tired of the old man's questioning. "An arrest warrant has been issued for Myriam. As soon as she has been apprehended then she will be brought back here to Castle Villeroy and executed along with her family."

"I see." Judge Strogen pondered this for a moment. "Then I am afraid that I cannot sign the order until her death has been confirmed. While Myriam lives she remains the rightful heir to the throne of Palara."

"Outrageous! What if she was confirmed as missing. She may very well be dead. No one has seen or heard from her for some days now. How could a young child survive, wandering the countryside alone? Could we not declare that she is missing and presumed dead, therefore no longer considered heir to the throne?"

"Absolutely," agreed the judge amiably. "There is certainly some precedent for that, and our laws are quite clear on how a situation like this should be handled. The period of absence that must be observed is set at seven years. You would be appointed as Regent of the Kingdom, but Myriam must be missing for at least seven years before you could be crowned as King."

"Damn these foolish laws!" cursed Harald, the large vein in his neck throbbing fiercely and his face turning a worryingly red color.

"I'm sorry sir, I can't see any way around this difficult situation," said the judge holding out the palms of his hands.

"What if I had you killed?" Duke Harald had a steely glint in his eye. "What if I had you killed and all of your fellow judges? What if I rewrote the laws of this kingdom? What if I declared myself King? Placed the crown on my own head and ruled this country like a man? Like my forefathers? Like the Great Chief Terrick did when he united the tribes and formed this great nation!"

"I humbly urge you to respect our laws and traditions sir," insisted the judge. "It is our laws and traditions that have kept our country safe and secure throughout the years that have passed since the Great Flood."

"Get out!" shouted Harald. "Get out! Get out! Get out!" Harald stood up suddenly and tipped over the table at which they were sitting, sending the jug of wine and goblets spinning across the floor, causing the old judge to fall backwards off his chair. The judge hurriedly picked himself up and scurried out of the throne room, thankful to have escaped with his head still attached to his shoulders. He had always heard that Duke Harald had a terrible temper, but he had never seen it in action before.

As the door slammed shut behind the departing judge, Harald threw himself sullenly into the wooden throne, the throne that he coveted, the throne that would soon belong to him. He just had to be patient. It was just a matter of time. He was concerned that he hadn't yet heard from Henrickson, his captain of the guard. Perhaps it had been foolish to send him off to Vandemland, but it had seemed a relatively simple mission.

Impatience was one of Harald's faults. Always rushing on to the next big idea instead of seeing through the challenges that had to be faced. He hadn't expected that seizing the throne would be so difficult. He had the support of the army, and he had the support of the nobles. It infuriated him that he was being outwitted by a girl.

Now, his ambitions were being blocked by a frail old judge in black, silk robes. Harald was torn, his heart told him to defy convention, to defy laws and rules and everything that stood in his way. But his head told him that he had to try and bide his time, that unless he was crowned King according to the laws and customs of the land then everything that he had worked so hard for could quickly unravel. He needed to be patient. He needed to let time run its course. Unfortunately patience and time were two things that he did not have a lot of.

CHAPTER 25

"You're mad!" hissed Ragnald. "You'll never make it!"

"I have to try!" whispered Henrickson. "Come with me!" Ragnald shook his head, unwilling to risk his life on the slim hope of escaping from the soldiers that guarded the mines of Vandemland.

Henrickson had waited until nightfall. As the sun began to set, the guards finally called an end to the working day and led the slaves, shackled by chains around their ankles, back to their sleeping quarters. The sleeping quarters were rows of canvas tents set back from the top of the mine. Six slaves to each tent. Conditions were crowded, dirty, there were fleas, and an inescapable stench that seemed to permeate everything. Henrickson had spent the first few days of his captivity trying to find a weak point in the mine's security, trying to figure out how he could possibly escape from this hell-hole and return to Palara.

Henrickson felt that the slaves were too closely observed during the day for there to be any chance of avoiding detection, but at night when they were all chained together in their tents there might be some hope of sneaking past the guards.

The first thing that he had to do was to get the chain off from around his ankle. It was a thick, rusted, iron chain, fixed to him by a manacle. He'd concealed a sharp piece of rock in his clothing while working down in the mine. As soon as they had been marched into their tent he used the rock to begin working away at the manacle, banging the rock against the rusted joint, and using brute force to try and free himself from the chains that bound him. Several times his blows missed the iron manacle and the rock painfully struck his leg, blood flowing from the wound.

"Do it quietly," whispered Ragnald. "You will bring the guards here and they will kill us all!"

"Shut up coward," spat Henrickson. "Your fate is no concern of mine." Eventually the hinge on the manacle broke beneath the pressure of the rock and the chains fell from Henrickson's ankle. His next challenge was to somehow move away from the tented camp where the slaves spent each night. The tents were arranged in long rows, with guards patrolling up and down in between each row.

Henrickson tried to peer out through the flap in the tent. The visibility was poor but he could just make out a guard walking down towards them. Henrickson pulled his head back inside and waited until the guard passed. Once the coast was clear he quickly slid out of the tent and crouched down behind it. There was a guard patrolling in front of him and a guard patrolling behind. He needed to evade their detection and make it to the perimeter of the camp. The boundary was also patrolled, but under cover of darkness Henrickson felt that he had a chance of escape.

He crawled low on his belly, pausing in the shadows as the guards came close, moving only when the coast was clear, slowly but surely making his way to the perimeter. When he reached the end of the edge of the camp he stood up and began to move slowly towards the fence line where the guards patrolled.

It was a cloudy night, the stars were barely visible, and Henrickson had to almost feel his way across the dry rocky ground. He paused. He could see one patrol to his left and one patrol to his right. If he moved quickly he had a clear path directly in front. Henrickson moved cautiously forward, one foot in front of the other, ears pricked for any sign of movement from the watching patrols. Henrickson's heart was racing, his adrenalin pumping as his hopes began to rise of a successful escape. He hadn't made any sort of plan for where he would go or how he would attempt to make the journey back to Palara. His mind was solely focused on escaping from the captivity of the mine first. Slowly, cautiously, one foot in front of the other.

Suddenly there was the sound of a dull metal click and Henrickson's body was flooded with searing biting pain. He couldn't hold back the scream that roared involuntarily from his lungs. He looked down and saw the metal teeth of the trap biting into his leg, the blood flooding from the gaping wound as the steel jaws firmly held his leg within its grasp. He tried to wrestle the jagged teeth of the trap open, desperately trying to free himself, but the next thing he felt was a thud to the back of his head, knocking him unconscious.

It was morning when Henrickson was woken by the bucket of cold water thrown on his face. He groaned, the pain in his leg was unbearable. Before he knew what was happening he was dragged out into the middle of the camp where all the slaves were being assembled before beginning their day of work. Henrickson was thrown down into the dust, in agonizing pain from the wound in his leg, the searing sun making it almost impossible to see.

"Let this be a lesson to you all!" shouted the guard that was standing over Henrickson's crumpled body. "No one escapes from the mines of Vandemland! No one! You are all slaves here and you will die here, as slaves!"

Chains were wrapped around Henrickson's ankles and wrists and he was stretched out painfully. The guard pulled a long blade out from the scabbard on his belt and held it aloft so that the assembled slaves could appreciate the punishment that was about the be meted out. The blade flashed brilliantly in the rays of the sun as it made its first cut across Henrickson's abdomen, slicing his body open. He was barely conscious, beyond registering any more pain, beyond feeling anything as the second cut of the knife sliced down his body lengthways, the blood gathering in a pool around him.

"Bring forth the slaves who shared this vermin's tent last night!" roared the guard, wiping Henrickson's blood from his dagger. Ragnald and the other four men were pushed roughly forward. "Kneel!" instructed the guard. The five slaves knelt in a line, facing the broken body of the dying Henrickson. One by one, the guard stood behind each of the kneeling slaves, grabbing hold of the hair on their head and pulling them back so that their neck was exposed. He then sliced his sharp blade across each of their throats, swiftly ending their lives, and their captivity. Ragnald was the last in line. He knew what was coming, and he almost looked forward to it. Finally able to put an end to this torture, this wretched existence. Finally, freedom.

CHAPTER 26

"Once we have passed through the fort then we will need to leave the main road as soon as we can," instructed Zander as his small company of men passed through the border crossing from the Berghein Valley into the Kingdom of Palara. The border was not tightly controlled. Two flags from the ruling houses marked each side. The flag of Castle Locke was a white horse on a green background, and on the opposing side the flag of the Kingdom of Palara was a golden eagle soaring over water.

To leave the Berghein Valley, Zander and his four men passed through a small guard post that was manned by the guard of the Duchess D'Anjue. The guards recognized Zander's insignia and his rank as chief counsel to the Duchess. The control barrier was immediately opened for them so that they could pass through unimpeded. On the other side of the border, the Kingdom of Palara had a small fort that was known as Forest Hill, as it stood at the top of a small rise giving views back across the Cefinon Forest and over the border into the Berghein Valley.

The fort had been built a long time ago. It was built from stone, designed to last and hold this strategic position for the Kingdom of Palara. There was a small troop of soldiers charged with holding the fort and monitoring any traffic that was passing in or out of the Berghein Valley.

"Halt!" challenged the guard, as Zander and his men approached. "State your business!"

"I am Zander Moncrieff, chief counsel to the Duchess D'Anjou. I travel on official business to Castle Villeroy."

"Show me your papers." Zander handed over his letter of passage that bore the seal of the Duchess D'Anjou. "Make sure you stick to the main road," said the soldier gruffly, handing back Zander's documents after studying them briefly. "There are bandits in the forest."

"Thank you, we will."

The soldiers opened the gates that the fort used to control the road, and Zander and his men rode through, passing by the old stone fort and beginning their quest to try and find the Princess Myriam.

"Let's stop at that inn ahead," pointed Zander. "We need to try and get some local knowledge of what other paths lead through the forest." Zander spurred his horse Samphire forward and led his four men to the small highway inn. A wooden sign swung back and forth in the gentle breeze proclaiming it proudly as the The Bull's Horn.

Zander had brought only four men with him because he knew that he needed to travel fast, and to try and avoid drawing too much attention to his quest. He had chosen four of his best men. They were strong, reliable, trustworthy, and intensely loyal. All four men were in there early thirties (as was Zander) and had served Zander since his first appointment as a commanding officer in the Castle Locke guard.

The five men rode around the back of the inn so that they could feed and water the horses. The ride from Castle Locke to the border, and then across into the Kingdom of Palara, had taken them all morning, so the horses were obviously pleased to be able to take a break.

"Good afternoon, gentlemen!" greeted the innkeeper coming out to the stables to welcome them. "Can I interest you in some lunch? We have some very tasty lamb shanks today. The meat is so tender that it falls off the bone and melts in your mouth."

"Yes, that sounds good, thank you. I'm sure we've all worked up an appetite," replied Zander. The innkeeper bustled around to pull five chairs around a table and poured them mugs of beer while the kitchen prepared their meals.

"And where are you heading to then?" asked the innkeeper, making conversation as he put their beers on the table. "By the look of your clothing I'd say that you've just come across from the Berghein Valley. What brings you to the Kingdom of Palara?"

Zander was always friendly with innkeepers. They were usually useful to pump for information. "We are on our way to Castle Villeroy. But we were also interested in seeing some of the forest, so we were wondering if there was another path that we could follow, away from the main road. Would you know of any?"

"Well, there are lots of paths into the forest, but no one really knows where they all lead or where they'll take you. Plus the soldiers have told us that there are a lot of bandits in this part of the forest and that we have to be extra vigilant. They've increased the number of men manning the fort as well."

"What about rivers or lakes in the area? Are there any major bodies of water that we should see?"

"Of course, the main river is the River Walsall which flows into the Damatine Sea at the port of Brammanville. You'll cross over the river when you get to Athaca on the main road, although I hear that the town was damaged recently in an attack."

Zander wondered if it had anything to do with the Princess. "An attack? What sort of attack?"

"Oh, I don't really know all the details," replied the innkeeper. "I only hear stories from soldiers and travelers, but apparently it was a gang of bandits that had been arrested in Athaca, but they managed to escape by setting the town on fire."

"Do you know anything about these bandits?"

"No, I'm afraid not, but the soldiers have increased their patrols to try and find them, so I'm sure it won't be long until they've been captured and executed. Enjoy your lunch gentlemen!"

CHAPTER 27

"I don't like this," growled Ganry, looking out through the small window in the room in which they had been locked by the lake men.

"Yes," agreed Artas, "it worries me that they have kept Myriam separate. Do you think that they will harm her?"

"It's hard to say. I've no experience of these lake men. They seem a pretty rough lot."

"There have been stories of the lake men," mused Barnaby. "No one was really sure that they existed, but there were always tales of tribes of people living deep in the forest. The tribes were here before the flood, and they resisted the great chief Terrick's wars to unite the kingdom."

"How have they stayed hidden for so long?" asked Hendon.

"Well, we are deep in the Cefinon Forest now, although I'm not exactly sure where we are..." pondered Barnaby. "I guess the only way to get here is along the

river that we drifted down and they probably kill anyone who comes across them by accident."

"Like us?" Artas was greatly concerned. "That
means that they will probably kill us, doesn't it?"

"Probably," sighed Barnaby. "If it means protecting
their home, and protecting their existence."

"It's funny though," said Ganry, still trying to see
out the window. "They seemed to know quite a bit
about the Kingdom of Palara. They knew enough about
the outside world to know what we were talking about."

Barnaby traced his hand along the wall of their cell.
"Yes, I noticed that. They are certainly not completely
primitive. It has taken a certain ingenuity to remain hidden for so long, to build a culture, a way of life that re-
volves completely around this isolated lake deep in the
forest. I imagine that they interrogate anyone that they
capture to obtain as much information as possible."

"Great," groaned Ganry, "they're going to torture us
first and *then* kill us. This is working out really well."
Ganry returned his attention to trying to scope out their
the surroundings of their prison. He could see that it
was a small fishing village, all made of wood, the
houses and buildings constructed on stilts out across the
water, which were connected by wooden walkways and
pontoons that formed a small marina. He couldn't see a
lot of people in the village, and no real sign of any
guards. Mostly just men that seemed to belong to the
boats of the fishing fleet. "This is only an outpost."

"What do you mean?" asked Artas, joining Ganry at
the window.

"They don't really live here, that's why it feels so rough and temporary," explained Ganry. "I think it's just some sort of fishing outpost for them."

"So there is another settlement somewhere? On this lake also?"

"I guess so, but who knows?" shrugged Ganry. "We really don't know what we're dealing with here. If Barnaby's theory is correct, we might never know. They might interrogate and kill us here before we even see their main settlement."

Artas clenched his fists. "Then we will need to escape."

"This way, Princess," said Clay, the chief of the lake men, stepping down into the small boat that was secured to the wooden pontoon outside his residence. He held out his hand to help Myriam to follow him down. It was a simple, wooden boat that was functional, but had some trappings that indicated that this was a boat that belonged to someone of importance. There was a small sail that helped to catch the breeze and there were several oarsmen that helped to guide the boat away from the pontoon. Myriam looked back towards the wooden settlement where she knew her companions remained imprisoned. She felt sick at being separated from Ganry, Artas, Hendon, and Barnaby, but she felt that she didn't have a choice. This was the only way that she would be able to save them.

Myriam sat down on the wooden bench, and hugged herself tight. "Where are we going?"

"To my city, Halawa," replied Clay proudly. "It's not far, just across the lake."

"But what of my companions?"

"It is better that they remain at the fishing village. Safer for them. And safer for you."

Myriam pulled her cloak around her shoulders and shivered, partly from the cold wind generated by the speed of the boat across the lake, but mostly from fear of the unknown, of what might lie ahead.

Myriam studied Clay, the chief of the lake men. He stood in the bow of the boat, clearly in charge of the crew, carefully scanning the waters ahead, a man at home on the water, a man that was at one with this lake. He looked to be in his late 40s, but it was hard to tell, as his face was weathered, and his body was strong. His hair was long, tied at the back, streaked with gray. His beard was also streaked with gray, plaited at the ends. His clothing was made from a dull material, a long cloak billowed behind him. The crew of his boat were dressed similarly. They were tall, proud men. Lake men.

CHAPTER 28

Queen Alissia was awoken by the sound of key, turning slowly in a lock. She stirred on the uncomfortable bed in the dungeon cell in which she and her husband King Ludwig had been locked since Duke Harald seized control. It was early, still well before sunrise, and the dungeon was pitch black. The Queen sat up and tried to peer out into the darkness to see what was going on. She heard another key slowly turning in a lock. She quickly shook her husband who was lying next to her.

"What is it?" he asked, opening his eyes.

"Someone is coming," whispered the Queen. She could see the flickering of a torch beginning to throw some light into the dungeon as its holder made their way down the steep stone stairs. "It's the dungeon master," said the Queen, watching intently as the bulky shape of the brutish man used the torch that he was carrying to begin lighting other torches around the dungeon.

"It's the middle of the night? What do you think he's doing here?" asked the King. Just then there was the sound of voices and the rattle of armed men descending the stairs.

"Soldiers!" exclaimed the Queen, immediately getting out of bed and wrapping herself in her cloak. "They could be coming for us," she said, handing the King his cloak. The Queen peered out of the small barred window of their cell, looking out into the dungeon to try and work out what was going on. A company of six armed soldiers were standing to attention, waiting. More footsteps were heard as someone else began the descent into the dungeon.

"It's Judge Strogen!" whispered the Queen as the elderly Chief Judge of Palara emerged into sight.

"I don't like this," grumbled the King. "Why would they have dragged the Chief Judge down here in the middle of the night?"

The Queen watched as the judge spoke briefly to the dungeon master who then picked up his ring of keys. The dungeon master led the judge across to one of the cells, but he didn't approach the cell that contained the King and Queen. Instead he went to the adjacent cell that imprisoned Lord Holstein and his wife Elisabeth.

The Queen tried to watch and listen as the cell door was opened. The judge spoke quietly. "Lord Holstein and Lady Holstein. You have been imprisoned in these dungeons because you have both been charged with treason. In my capacity as Chief Judge of the Kingdom of Palara, I hereby find you guilty as charged and sentence you to death. Your execution will be carried out immediately." The Queen closed her eyes as she heard

Lady Holstein begin screaming and wailing in horror as the reality of the judge's pronouncement hit her. The guards stepped forward to surround Lord and Lady Holstein to lead them from their cell.

"I forbid this! I forbid this!" shouted the King angrily. "Judge Strogen! I am still the rightful King of Palara and you have no authority to make this judgment or pass this sentence. I forbid this, do you hear me!" The judge did not acknowledge the King in any way, but slowly and carefully led the way out of the dungeon and up the steep stone steps, with the guards escorting Lord and Lady Holstein following behind. As they watched the lights of the torches slowly disappearing, and heard the last of the doors being locked, the Queen broke down and sobbed as the King wrapped his arms around her.

"It's only a matter of time before they kill us too, isn't it," she said sadly.

"We can only pray to the gods now," replied the King. "Pray for some kind of miracle."

As the sun slowly began to rise to the east of Castle Villeroy, a single drummer began to beat a muted rhythm in one of the small courtyards within the Castle. Duke Harald took a seat on the plain wooden chair that had been placed for him on the gray flagstones, so that he could observe proceedings.

The soldiers led Lord and and Lady Holstein out into the center of the courtyard where a block of wood had been positioned. This is where the Kingdom of Palara executed people by beheading them. Execution by beheading was a punishment reserved for members of the nobility, or prisoners of some political or religious importance. Ordinary criminals simply had their throats cut by the local Sheriff, but the execution of someone of noble birth required a bit more ceremony.

Judge Strogen stood in front of the executioner's wooden block. The executioner, wearing a black hood and clutching his axe, stood patiently to one side.

"I, Judge Strogen, the Chief Judge of the Kingdom of Palara, hereby authorize the execution of Lord Holstein and Lady Holstein," announced the judge, as loud as his frail voice would carry.

The judge stepped to one side and a priest stepped forward to say a prayer over the prisoners. The judge nodded to the soldiers who led Lady Holstein towards the executioner's block. She was ghostly white, her face pale, her eyes red from crying. Her whole body seemed numb. She knelt down and placed her neck on the block of wood, her chin in the groove that had been specially carved for the purpose.

Lord Holstein, unable to watch, closed his eyes as he saw the executioner move into position. The executioner slowly raised his heavy iron axe and then brought it swiftly down, the blade slicing cleanly through the long, elegant neck of Lady Holstein. As he heard the thud of the axe blade hitting the wood, Lord Holstein's body shuddered. He felt sick to his very core. As the soldiers grabbed hold of his arms, he opened his eyes and saw his wife's lifeless body being unceremoniously dragged away.

"You will pay for these crimes!" he shouted bitterly at Duke Harald who was watching proceedings with apparent disinterest.

"My dear Lord Holstein," smirked Harald, "I'm afraid that it is you who are about to pay for your crimes."

Lord Holstein was led to the executioner's wooden block, freshly stained with the blood of his wife. He knelt down and placed his chin in the groove carved into the block, closing his eyes in an attempt to block out the ugly reality of what was about to happen. The hooded executioner slowly raised up his iron axe and then quickly brought the sharp blade down onto Lord Holstein's exposed neck, cleanly severing his head from his shoulders, creating a pool of blood that surrounded the block of wood that had ended the lives of so many.

"Very good." Harald stood up from his chair and stretched his arms. "I think it might rain today?" he said, examining the dark clouds that were forming in sky, before striding off back inside the castle, hastily followed by his retinue of guards and attendants.

CHAPTER 29

"You will be sleeping in the slave quarters at the back of the villa, but most of your time will be spent here in the main house," explained Badr al Din, the chief housekeeper who had purchased Arexos from the Vandemland slave market.

Arexos followed the housekeeper in a daze. He was still having difficulty understanding how he now found himself in this position. It seemed only moments ago that he was traveling with his master Henrickson, the captain of the guard at Castle Villeroy. They had paid the Narc smugglers to transport them into Vandemland, but once the blindfolds had been removed, it was clear that the Narcs had betrayed them, deciding to sell them into slavery as retribution for the difficulties that the soldiers of Palara had caused to their smuggling operations.

Arexos had been pulled from the horse that he had been riding, the blindfold untied, and then chained to a post while the Narc's negotiated his sale to the highest bidder. He had seen his master Henrickson being dragged off and thrown onto a cart with other slaves. He had tried to call out to Henrickson but one of the Narcs had slapped him across the face to silence him.

Arexos hadn't been able to follow the negotiations that had been swirling around him, but before too long he had been unchained from the post where he was standing and led along to a horse drawn cart. The man that had bought him was Badr al Din, the chief house-keeper who was now patiently explaining the operations of the villa and what Arexos's duties would entail.

"Any questions?" asked Badr al Din with a warm smile.

"Um… who owns the villa?" asked Arexos uncertainly.

"The man that owns this villa, and the man that now owns you, is Qutaybah, one of the most powerful men in Vandemland."

"And this is his home?"

"One of his homes!" laughed Badr al Din. "He mainly uses this villa as a hunting lodge, so he may come and stay for a few weeks at a time, often bringing a lot of people with him that he will entertain. He's not here at the moment, but we are expecting him to arrive in the next few days. That is why we have had to in-crease the staff in readiness. That is why we have bought you."

"Oh, I see…" Arexos said stiffly. "Are you a slave too?"

"You're very inquisitive for a young boy!" chortled Badr al Din. "Yes, of course I'm a slave. Almost every-one in Vandemland is a slave of some sort. Only the noble families are free citizens of these lands, the rest of us all belong to them. You my dear boy, as a slave captured from a conquered people, are the lowest status level of all slaves, the lowest of the low."

"But I'm not from a conquered people!" protested Arexos. "I'm from the Kingdom of Palara. Vandemland hasn't conquered Palara."

"That is of no importance," dismissed Badr al Din. "You were sold in a slave market by slave traders, that means you are a conquered slave, the lowest of the low."

"Were you a conquered slave too?"

"No indeed I was not!" snorted Badr al Din. "My family were shepherd's on the grasslands owned by Qutaybah's family. I was very fortunate to be selected to join the household staff. Only tradesmen and merchants are of a higher cast than shepherds. Now enough talk, let's get you bathed and dressed in some fresh clothes. You may be a captured slave, but you at least need to look a bit presentable."

Arexos meekly followed Badr al Din, who led the way into the bathing room attached to the sleeping quarters for the slaves. It was a simple but functional stone pool of hot water with jugs of cold water filled from a nearby aqueduct.

"How does it work?" asked Arexos, looking at the bath in confusion.

"Take your dusty clothes off, rinse the dirt off you with the cold water, and then you soak your body in the warm tub, and then before you put your robes on you apply this oil to your skin," explained Badr al Din patiently.

Arexos sniffed at the jug suspiciously. "What's the oil?"

"It's just almond oil. It's good for your body, keeps you healthy. Hurry up now, we have chores to do!"

Arexos quickly stepped out of his clothes, sluiced himself with the cold water to wash the dust and smell of the slave market away, before sliding into the warm water of the bathing pond.

"Oh, this is nice…" sighed Arexos appreciatively, suddenly forgetting the stress and anxiety that had been overwhelming him, the warm water soaking his tired body.

"Come on now, you're not here to enjoy yourself!" scolded Badr al Din, holding a cloth out to Arexos so that he could dry the water from himself as he emerged from the bath. "Smear the oil onto your skin and put this robe on. This will be what you wear now that you are part of the staff here at Villa Salamah."

CHAPTER 30

Zander pushed his chair back from the table and threw his cloak around his shoulders. "Right boys, let's saddle up and get moving."

It had been a hearty lunch at The Bull's Horn inn and a good chance to refresh the horses after their ride this morning from Castle Locke, but every minute was precious if they were going to be successful in their search for Princess Myriam.

"Sir, the attack on Athaca that the innkeeper was talking about, do you think that has anything to do with Myriam?" asked Aban, one of Zander's men.

"It's about the only lead that we have so far. We might need to take a gamble on it. It would certainly help to narrow our search as it would place her somewhere between Athaca and here."

"But she wouldn't be traveling on the main road," chipped in Yasir, another of Zander's men, as they rode along. "So she's either gone north into the farmlands that lie towards the coast or she's gone South into the Cefinon Forest."

"Yes, that's true, Yasir," acknowledged Zander. "I can't imagine that she will have gone into the forest though. There's no way that she could navigate her way through that, so my guess is that she will be trying to pass through the farmlands without drawing attention to herself."

"But sir, remember that the innkeeper spoke of brigands. It almost sounded like a gang of some sort. Perhaps she isn't traveling alone, perhaps she is with companions? In that case a group of them is more likely to attract attention in the farmlands, and she may have someone with her that knows the forest, which would make that a safer option."

"I hadn't thought of it like that. We could try splitting up so that we try and cover both scenarios, but at this stage I'd prefer us to stick together, if possible. The trouble is, if they've gone into the forest, they really could be anywhere, and the Duchess's visions of water don't seem to be helping us, unless she was perhaps referring to the River Walsall at Athaca?"

"So what are your orders, sir?" Aban was eager to proceed.

"Let's take the first path into the forest that we can find," decided Zander. "I'm not sure where this search will take us, but we'll just need to keep trying to gather information as we progress. Yasir, you and Najid ride ahead and scout us a path off this road and into the forest."

Yasir and Najid spurred their horses on and cantered away. Zander studied the road ahead and the trees that were becoming thick on each side of the road. This main road led to the town of Athaca, across the River Walsall. It then went all the way across the Kingdom of Palara to Castle Villeroy, becoming the main east-west transport link for the country. From Athaca north to the Damatine Sea, the main transport link was the River Walsall, which carried timber and goods down to the port of Brammanville where the Kingdom's fleet was harbored. The east/west road effectively bordered the Cefinon Forest which lay to the south of the road, thick forest all the way to the foot of the Basalt Mountains.

Zander was not looking forward to entering into the forest. He had heard stories, fairytales mostly. There were legends of wild beasts, monsters, and tribes of un-tamed men who did not bow to the laws of civilized man. He hoped that somewhere in that forest was Prin-cess Myriam, and that somehow she was still safe.

"Do you know this forest at all, Karam?" Zander asked the man riding beside him. Karam shook his head. Karam was one of Zander's most ferocious fight-ers. A mute, his tongue had been cut out as a child. "The stories... do you believe any of them?" Karam shrugged his shoulders.

"You're not scared are you, sir?" asked Aban.

"Not scared, Aban. Not scared, just a bit curious. Plus I don't really like surprises."

At that moment, Yasir and Najid came galloping back towards them.

"We need to get off the road now, sir!" shouted Yasir. "A large company of soldiers from the Kingdom of Palara, coming this way! Follow me, there's a path into the forest just ahead!" Zander and the others quickly broke into a canter and followed Yasir off the road and into the forest, along the small dirt path that soon seemed to be swallowed up by the surrounding trees. "They have dogs with them, sir. Let's push in deep as quickly as we can, we don't want to give them any reason to follow us. We'd be outnumbered if things got a bit sticky." They spurred the horses on, dodging low-hanging branches and vines as they sped along the forest path.

"We don't have a lot of daylight left." Zander and his men slowed their horses into a more sustainable speed. "We should think about making camp for the night. What about this clearing up ahead? Karam, you're in charge of finding some food, Yasir and Najid can take care of the horses, and Aban and I will get a fire going. We'll need to set a watch through the night."

Zander's men quickly set about their tasks, securing the horses, and gathering wood. It wasn't long before Karam returned with enough pigeons to feed them all, expertly dressing them and skewering them on sticks so that they could be roasted over the coals of the fire. As night fell they quickly made their beds and tried to get some sleep.

Zander took the first watch, sitting by the fire and silently observing the dark forest that surrounded them. The rustling in the branches, the impassive trees, the gnawing sense that someone or something was watching their every move.

CHAPTER 31

"Nearly there!" shouted Clay, chief of the Lake Men, turning back over his shoulder to smile encouragingly at Myriam, as the small boat sped across the still waters of the lake. Myriam nodded, and pulled her cloak tightly around her shoulders. As the boat rounded a tree-covered promontory, Myriam gasped as an enormous city came into view. Hundreds of elaborate wooden houses, built on stilts out over the water of the lake.

"This is Halawa!" beamed Clay, gesturing expansively.

Myriam looked around in awe. "I had no idea it would be so big."

"Yes, this is our main city, our main settlement."

The boat was soon pulling smoothly into dock against one of the many wooden pontoons. Clay was met by a small retinue, who appeared to be household staff. He held out his hand and assisted Myriam to step from the boat onto the pontoon. "Come, my home is this way!"

As they walked along, Clay was warmly greeted and welcomed by everyone who observed their approach. It was clear that Clay was a popular leader of the lake men. The wooden walkways that they followed led them towards a large building, long and low in its construction. As they walked towards it the doors swung open.

"Here we are!" smiled Clay, encouraging Myriam forward as he acknowledged the members of his household that were bowing in greeting, showing the appropriate respect to the chief of the lake men. "Let me introduce you. Everyone, this is Princess Myriam from the Kingdom of Palara. Princess, this is my sister Lisl and her son, my nephew Linz."

"Pleased to meet you," greeted Myriam politely.

"You are most welcome in our home," bowed Lisl. "Please, join us for refreshments by the fishpond."

Myriam followed Lisl who led the way through what Myriam assumed would be a palace. Clay's home was constructed of wood and it was a big open space. There didn't really seem to be any rooms or internal walls. There were some small partitions and curtains to create privacy or screen off certain sections, but as a home it seemed more like an enormous hall, quite different to Castle Villeroy where Myriam had grown up. The fishpond that Lisl had referred to was an intriguing space within the palace. There was a large round hole in the floor through which the water of the lake lapped quietly. There were seats around the hole and Myriam could see large, brightly colored fish swimming slowly around in the pond.

"I've never seen fish like these," admired Myriam. "Can they not swim away into the lake?"

"We have created a cage beneath the water so they can't really swim away," explained Lisl. "Plus we feed them so well that I don't think they would go anywhere even if there was no cage."

"What sort of fish do you call them?" asked Myriam, intrigued by their bright colors, long whiskers, and sharp teeth.

"They are Polopon fish. Don't put your fingers in the water as they are quick to bite. Beautiful but deadly, like so much in this world." Myriam drank the tea that was poured for her and ate some of the smoked fish that had been prepared. She looked across at Linz, Clay's nephew. He seemed quiet and reserved. She thought perhaps he was just shy.

"How old are you, Linz?" Myriam asked, trying to make conversation.

"Thirteen." He was barely able to meet Myriam's gaze.

"One day he will be chief of the tribe," beamed Clay, proudly slapping Linz on the back, seeming to cause him further embarrassment.

"You have no children of your own?" Myriam asked Clay.

"No, I have never married. I always seem to have been too busy to find a wife, but I am happy for my nephew to continue the family tradition and keep our tribe strong and prosperous."

"What are you doing here?" asked Linz quietly, shyly looking up at Myriam.

"There is trouble in my Kingdom. I am in hiding with my companions and I'm afraid that we stumbled upon your lake by accident."

Lisl looked across at Clay in alarm. "You have companions?"

"They are being held securely by the fishing fleet," soothed Clay.

"Please, will you release them?" Myriam pleaded. "I am worried that they will be hurt or mistreated, or that they may try and escape."

"It is really for their own protection that we are holding them there," replied Clay. "Our laws require that any outsiders who enter our lake must be immediately executed in order to keep our existence secret, in order to keep us safe. If we brought them here to Halawa I would have no choice but to order them to be killed. By keeping them with the fishing fleet out near the mouth of the river, we can avoid drawing too much attention to them, for a short time at least."

"Why have you brought me here then? Don't the laws apply to me also?"

Clay looked at Myriam thoughtfully, glancing briefly at his nephew. "I would like you to marry Linz. I would like you to remain here with us and become part of my family."

Myriam gasped and also noticed that Linz had opened his eyes wide in astonishment.

"But I can't stay here!" insisted Myriam. "I have to rescue my family and my kingdom. I have to find a way to take the throne to which I am the rightful heir!"

Clay was unmoved. "But my dear Princess. You must understand that now that you have found us, now that you have discovered our existence, we can never let you leave."

CHAPTER 32

"If only there was such a thing as magic," mused the Duchess D'Anjue, absent-mindedly twisting the thick, solid ring that she wore on the middle finger of her left hand. It had been several days now and still there had been no word from Zander, her chief counsel, who she had despatched to search for her missing granddaughter. The Duchess regretted not having been able to spend more time with Myriam, but she had tried to provide support from a distance, sending the learned Leonidavus to the Castle Villeroy to tutor Myriam and watch over her.

"It wasn't enough," muttered the Duchess, scolding herself. When Duke Harald had seized control of the Kingdom of Palara she had begun to lose hope. "I should never have tried to bargain with that fool."

The Duchess prided herself on her diplomacy and her ability to steer powerful men to follow the course that was most advantageous to her, and to her small principality within the Berghein Valley. Alissia was her youngest daughter and the match with Ludwig, the heir to the throne of Palara, had seemed too good to pass up, securing an alliance with her biggest neighbor, garnering the protection of the powerful armies of Palara.

Alissia had been a smart girl. She knew that marrying Ludwig was the right thing to do. Ludwig clearly wasn't the smartest of men, but he didn't seem to be overly violent and he wasn't unpleasant to look at.

When Myriam had been born, the Duchess insisted that Myriam be sent to her at Castle Locke, for schooling and tutorship, but Ludwig, King by this stage, flatly refused, demanding that as Myriam was the heir to the throne that she must remain in Palara at Castle Villeroy. Only after much beseeching by Alissia did he begrudgingly accept a tutor from Castle Locke.

Correspondence with Alissia had been infrequent, and the Duchess had only made the journey to Castle Locke once - for Myriam's twelfth birthday, an important occasion in the Berghein Valley.

The Duchess smoothed a gold thread that trailed across her robe as she walked to the window of her study, looking out across the valley below. She had never felt more alone. She had never felt more isolated. Her brow furrowed in thought.

Suddenly, as if she had reached some sort of clarity or decision, she reached out and rang the small bell that sat discretely on her desk.

Her valet opened the door of the study. "Yes, Your Excellence?"

"Send the captain of the guard to me."

The Duchess sat down at her desk. It was a simple design, made from the wood of the walnut trees that grow throughout the Berghein Valley. She picked up one of the scrolls that sat neatly on top of the desk, rolling it out in front of her so that she could study it closely. The Duchess was not a young woman, but her eyesight was still keen. With her index finger she traced the road that led from the Berghein Valley across the Kingdom of Palara, all the way to Castle Villeroy. To the south of the road lay the rich farmland that stretched to the coastline of the Damatine Sea, while to the north of the road lay the Cefinon Forest - the deep dark forest about which so little was known. The Duchess's concentration was disturbed by a polite knock on the door.

"Yes?"

"The Captain of the Guard is here to see you, Your Excellence," announced her valet.

"Thank you, send him in," commanded the Duchess. "Captain Versance, thank you for coming at such short notice," smiled the Duchess, greeting her captain.

"I am at your command, Your Excellence," bowed the captain. "How can I be of assistance?"

"What is the status of our army?"

"As we are in a time of peace we have stood down all but the permanent guards that protect the castle."

"How many men could we call up if we needed to?"

The captain looked concerned. "Are we under threat, Your Excellence?"

"Answer my questions first, captain," scolded the Duchess, "and then we will decide whether we are under threat. How many men could we call up if we needed to?"

The captain replied without hesitation. "Two thousand, Your Excellence."

"And how quickly could we have them called to arms and ready for action?"

"One week, Your Excellence," replied the captain confidently.

"Thank you captain, as always I am impressed by your command of our forces. You have always served me well."

"Your Excellence, what is the threat that we are facing?"

"War is coming captain. I don't know exactly when it will come, or where our greatest dangers lie, but I am certain that war is coming to the Berghein Valley."

"Would you like me to mobilize our forces?" asked the captain, uncertainly.

The Duchess didn't hesitate. "Yes. Call the men to arms. Every man that can wield a sword. The enemies that we will face will be stronger than us, they will be better trained than us, they will have more weapons than us. It is going to take all of our courage, all of our strength of will, to survive the storm that is bearing down on Castle Locke."

"Yes Your Excellence, I understand, I will see to it at once." The captain bowed deeply before leaving the room.

The Duchess returned to the window of her study, looking out over her estate. She felt a strange sense of foreboding. She wondered if any of them would survive the wrath of the Kingdom of Palara, whether any of them would survive the wrath of Duke Harald - the pretender to the throne.

CHAPTER 33

"These will be your quarters!" announced Clay, leading Myriam to a spacious room within the long, low wooden building which housed Clay and his household. "That is until you are married to Linz, and then we will set up something more comfortable, more suitable for my heir and his wife."

"Please, sir!" begged Myriam. "Please don't do this."

"This is your home now," replied Clay sternly. "There is nothing for you beyond this lake. My guards will be watching you, although should you try and escape there is no where for you to go. You would not survive one night out here in this jungle."

The chief of the lake men drew the curtain and left Myriam alone in her new quarters. The room was simply furnished but comfortable, a wooden floor covered by mats, a seating area with cushions, a sleeping area with furs and skins for warmth. Myriam could hear the gentle lapping of the waters of the lake beneath the wooden floor. To one side, there was a small water-wheel turning, a gentle stream of liquid passing through it, delivering fresh water to the room. Myriam admired its ingenuity before crossing the floor to the small window that looked out across the lake. She sighed deeply, frustrated at lurching from one danger to the next, worrying about the fate of Ganry, Artas, Hendon and Barnaby. She felt tears begin to roll down her cheeks. She brushed them away quickly, angry with herself for not being stronger, but the tears continued to fall as the fear and exhaustion began to take hold of her.

"Hello?" said a quiet, tentative voice, suddenly breaking through Myriam's misery. It was Linz, the chief's nephew, the boy she appeared to be destined to marry, the heir to the man who held her captive. "I'm sorry to disturb you," began Linz, but seeing that Myriam had been crying the boy seemed to have second thoughts and became embarrassed. "Oh I'm so sorry, I'll come back later."

"No, it's okay," said Myriam, drying her eyes and forcing herself to look Linz in the eye. "You may enter."

"Um, my uncle said that I should come and talk with you," mumbled Linz.

"And what did your uncle tell you that you should talk to me about?" asked Myriam, almost amused by the boy's lack of confidence and discomfort in her presence.

"He didn't say," replied Linz timidly.

Myriam crossed her arms. "Linz, I can't marry you. I don't belong here. I belong in my own kingdom, with my own people. You must understand that."

"I didn't realize that there was anything beyond the lake, beyond the forest."

"There is a whole world beyond this forest!" exclaimed Myriam exasperatedly. "You don't want to marry me anyway, I can see it in your eyes!"

"What do you mean?" asked Linz, looking concerned. "My uncle says that I must."

"Why don't you marry one of the girls from your own people, from the people of the lake?"

"My uncle says that it is forbidden. He says that the heir of the lake people must always take a wife from the foreign tribes."

"Which means kidnapping someone and holding them against their will?" demanded Myriam angrily.

"I don't know, I've never really thought about it," replied Linz shyly.

"Look at me Linz," said Myriam softly, reaching out and taking Linz's hands in her own. "Look me in the eyes. In your heart, do you really want to marry me? Do you really want to spend the rest of your life with me? Do you really want to have children with me?"

Linz gulped uncertainly, trying his best to hold her steady gaze. "No. No I don't. But I can't disobey my uncle."

"Listen, you will be heir to the lake people whether you marry me or not," said Myriam, trying to think of a way to use Linz's lack of interest in her to her advantage. "Your uncle's plans to marry us is purely opportunistic. If I wasn't here then it wouldn't be an issue, so it is in both of our interests if you help me to escape."

"I can't do that!" hissed Linz nervously.

"I'm not asking you to kill anyone!" countered Myriam. "I just need you to help me find a way back to the fishing village where my friends are being held prisoner."

"You would need a boat and someone to sail it," said Linz, thinking through the logistics.

"You could sail it for me?" suggested Myriam.

"But even if you were to escape, where would you go?"

"We need to get to the Berghein Valley."

Linz looked doubtful. "I've never heard of that."

"North I think. We need to go North or North-West."

"Across the other side of the lake there is a channel that runs to the north, but it is forbidden to enter it."

"Forbidden for you perhaps, but not for me!" smiled Myriam excitedly, as the possibility of escape began to take shape.

"We will have to travel at night to avoid detection by my uncle and his guards."

"So we will go after sundown tonight?"

"But the water dragons come out at night, it would be too dangerous to try and reach the fishing village."

"What exactly are these water dragons?"

"They are bigger than a man with skin covered in leathery scales. No spear or arrow can harm them and they have fierce ferocious teeth. They swim through the water and can also walk on land," explained Linz.

"Would they attack the boat?"

"They have been known to, although it is not very common."

"Then we shall just have to try and avoid them. We go tonight. Agreed?"

Linz nodded and they shook hands to seal their bar-gain. "Agreed."

CHAPTER 34

"Bring me my horse!" ordered Duke Harald, storming out towards the stables.

"Sir, would you like to go hunting?" His arms-bearer followed at his heels, trying to gauge his master's mood.

"No, I would not like to go hunting!" spat Harald. "My best hunters are out trying to catch that elusive fool of a girl. If they can't manage to snare her then they would be no use trying to hunt a fox! No. I will ride to consult the Druids. I will go alone."

The Prince's horse was called Thawban. It was a name that meant companion or friend. Harald was beginning to feel that his horse was the only thing that he could trust. Thawban was a beautiful horse, standing tall and proud, his shining dark black coat shimmering as it caught the light. The stable boys quickly saddled the beast and prepared him to be ridden. Thawban began to impatiently paw the ground as he sensed the presence of the Duke, the saddle and reins a clear indication that he was about to be let out from the constraints of the stable, out into the fields that lay beyond Castle Villeroy.

"Are you sure you don't want someone to accompany you, sir?" asked Zaim, the arms-bearer.

"I'm sure, this is something that I have to do alone. No harm will come to me. I will return before nightfall."

Harald took hold of the reins of his horse, positioned his left foot in the stirrup, and pulled himself up into the saddle, swinging his right leg over and securing it into the other stirrup.

"Come Thawban! Hah! Hah!" Harald urged his horse into a brisk gallop and his soldiers quickly opened the gates of the castle as he rode through and out onto the open road. It felt good to be away, even just for a moment, the wind clearing his head as Thawban cantered easily along the dirt road that would lead them to the Druids' temple on the outskirts of the Cefinon Forest.

Harald reflected that his plan had seemed so simple, yet ever since the moment that he had imprisoned his brother the King and seized control of Castle Villeroy, he seemed to be blocked and frustrated at every turn. He had ordered the execution of Lord Holstein and his wife Elisabeth in desperation, seeking some way of advancing his claim on the throne, a claim that seemed to be impossible to fill while Myriam remained out of his reach.

After two hours of solid riding, Harald came within site of the Druids' temple - a small stone building being reclaimed by the forest, with creepers and grasses growing from every nook and cranny in the stone.

One of the slaves of the Druids helped Harald to dismount and led his horse Thawban away to the stables to be fed and watered. Harald walked towards the large wooden door that was the entrance to the temple. The door opened slowly and an elderly man came out, dressed in a white robe. He wore a garland of mistletoe around his head and carried a staff made from oak.

"We have been expecting you, Duke Harald."

"Your prophecies are false!" roared Harald. "I have followed everything that you have told me and yet still I am not king!"

"Then why do you return here if you do not seek our counsel?" asked the druid humbly, leading Harald through the small antechamber and into the larger hall concealed within the stone building.

The druid sat beside a small altar where a fire was burning. He poured some wine into an earthen goblet and gave it to Harald to drink.

"Did you bring a sacrifice in order for us to seek the guidance of the spirits?" inquired the druid.

Harald reached inside his cloak and pulled out a small flask, handing it to the druid. "It is the blood of Lord Holstein who I sacrificed in the name of the spirits."

"A fitting sacrifice," said the druid solemnly, taking the stopper from the flask and pouring a small amount of blood into a silver bowl that was being heated over the coals of the fire. "All human souls are immortal. Death is only temporary. We pass from one form to another."

The druid added some dried powders to the small silver bowl, swirling the blood gently as it heated. A strong odor began to fill the room and the druid closed his eyes.

"What do you see?" asked Harald eagerly.

"What questions do you seek answers to?" countered the druid.

"Will I be King?"

"There are many paths that could lead you to the crown. But these paths are not yet certain while the Princess Myriam remains the rightful heir."

"Does Myriam live?"

The druid swayed back and forth. "Yes. She lives, but her life is in danger. She has not reached safety."

"Where can I find her?" demanded the Duke.

"She is surrounded by water. Her heart looks to the west but her path is hidden from her."

"Surrounded by water? What does that mean? She escaped from Athaca, we know that. There is no other water between Athaca and the Berghein Valley?"

"She is trapped in the hidden lake, deep in the Cefinon Forest beyond your reach," said the druid.

"I will burn that forest to the ground if I have to!" snarled Harald. "Nothing is beyond my reach!"

The druid tipped the mixture of blood and powders into the burning flames of the fire, causing it to hiss and spark.

"What else do you see?" demanded Harald.

"You will bring death and destruction to us all," the druid said calmly, standing up and walking away into the darkness of the temple.

Harald was left staring at the embers of the fire, struggling to control the fury that burned so fiercely inside him.

CHAPTER 35

As daylight broke in the Cefinon forest, Zander stirred his four men. Param was in charge of preparing some breakfast for them all, which was a thick porridge paste made from mixing oats and water. He heated it over the small fire rekindled from the coals of the night before.

"I don't know how many days I can take of this miserable breakfast." Yasir forcibly spooned the porridge into his mouth.

"Stop complaining!" ordered Zander. "We've eaten worse. We're on a mission. There will be time enough for good food when we have found Myriam and returned her safely to her grandmother."

After finishing breakfast they gathered their belongings and untethered their horses.

"We're really working blind here, sir," said Aban, who had returned from scouting out ahead. "We can keep following this path, but we've really got no idea where it will take us. As far as I can see it goes further into the forest, but for how long is anyone's guess."

Zander shook his head wearily. "This is madness, isn't it?" His men realized it was a rhetorical question which did not require a response. Aban, Yasir, Najid, and Karam sat patiently on their horses, waiting for some sort of order or direction from their leader.

"I could help you," said a voice from behind them. Zander and his men quickly turned in surprise, hands clutching at the hilt of swords in readiness for a surprise attack.

"Who are you!" demanded Zander gruffly, staring down at the small man wearing a simple brown cassock.

"Well, that's not very polite is it!" replied the man. "I offer to help you and you start rattling your swords at me! Do you want my help or not?"

"Why would you help us?" asked Zander suspiciously.

"I'm just a good natured soul, I guess," laughed the man. "Clearly you don't need my help though, so I'll be on my way." The man picked up his rucksack and turned back along the path towards the main road.

"Wait," said Zander, realizing that there seemed to be no better options available. "We do need your help. Tell me your name, friend."

The man turned back around. "I am Ghaffar. I live in this forest."

"Are you a druid?"

"No," laughed Ghaffar, "they don't train men like me to become druids. I guess I'm something like a monk. Are you lost?"

"No, we're not lost," Zander said stiffly.

"Have you lost something, then?" probed Ghaffar.

"Perhaps." Zander considered his words carefully, not wanting to reveal too much to a stranger. "Yes, we are trying to determine the best way for us to search the forest for what we have lost."

Ghaffar cocked his head askance. "Do you search for the missing Princess Myriam?"

"What makes you say that?" asked Zander suspiciously. He was unsure what to make of this self proclaimed monk.

Ghaffar smiled broadly. "It seems that everyone searches for the Princess Myriam. From the soldiers of Duke Harald, to the waters of the River Walsall, to the trees of the forest, and yet she remains unfound."

"What do you mean by that? Are you able to help us with our search or not?"

"Well, that depends on why you search for Myriam. We know what Duke Harald intends to do to her, but the question is whether she would be safer with you, or safer to remain concealed within the trees of the Cefinon Forest."

"She will come to no harm with us. We are from the Berghein Valley, the land of her family, we will take her there to safety."

"There is no such thing as safety. Not here, not anywhere. Not anymore," said Ghaffar mysteriously.

"Sir, this fool is talking around us in circles!" growled Aban impatiently. "I say let us cut off his monkish head and be on our way."

"Calm yourself, Aban," counseled Zander. "It is often the way of lonely monks to talk just for the sake of talking. Without him we are back to square one." Zander took a deep breath and attempted once more to make some sense of what the monk was telling him. "Ghaffar the monk, you say that Myriam is concealed within the trees of the Cefinon Forest? The Duchess D'Anjou has had visions that she is surrounded by water. Are these riddles saying the same thing?"

"Ah, clever Duchess. She has not lost her powers after all. Yes, Zander Moncrieff, everyone knows where Myriam is hidden but no one can speak its name."

"How do you know who I am?!"

"There are no secrets from the trees of Cefinon Forest."

"Can you take us to this place? This place where Myriam is hidden?"

"I can show you the way," nodded Ghaffar, "but I am forbidden to cross the water."

"Well, that at least is something. Let's go."

"Sir, are you sure?" cautioned Aban. "This feels like some sort of deception."

"His timely assistance does seem too good to be true," agreed Zander in a whisper. "But without some sort of guidance we could be lost in this forest for the rest of time. Stay alert, stay on guard. We will need our wits about us." Zander held out his arm to Ghaffar to help pull him up onto the back of his horse, Samphire. "Which way, good monk?"

"Follow the path. The trees will show us the way."

CHAPTER 36

"Here's your food," said the lake man, as one of the guards opened the door to the room where Ganry and the others were being held.

As he placed the bowls of food on the floor, there was a dull thud as Ganry brought both his fists down onto the back of his head, knocking him unconscious. The clatter of the falling man and spilt bowls quickly brought the guards running. As they stormed through the door, Ganry and Artas worked together to knock them over, using brute force to push them off their feet.

"Sound the alarm!" came a cry from outside. "The prisoners are trying to escape! All hands to the pier!" Guards came running thick and fast. Despite their best efforts, Ganry and Artas were soon overwhelmed, and all four of the prisoners were secured in tightly bound ropes.

"Well boys, we gave it a shot," apologized Ganry.

"Silence!" shouted the guard standing over them.

"I was just telling my friends," began Ganry, but he was cut short by a sharp blow across the face from the angry-looking guard, eagerly repaying Ganry for the blows he had suffered during the prisoner's break-out attempt.

"You have no right to speak!" snarled the guard. "We should kill them now!" yelled the guard to one of the men who seemed to be in charge.

"Those are not our orders," replied the man. "We are to keep them secure until we receive word from Clay as to their fate. In the meantime they can remain tied in ropes so that there are no more escape attempts."

"A boat approaches," shouted a look-out. "From the Halawa direction."

"Unusual for anyone to be out in the water at night. Is it Clay?"

"It flies the symbol of Clay's house, but it's not his boat," reported the look-out, peering into the darkness of the night.

"You must stay hidden," whispered Linz, helping Myriam to conceal herself in the bottom of the boat beneath several old cloaks. "Do not move until I come for you." Linz expertly guided his boat into dock on one of the floating piers of the fishing outpost.

"Who goes there!" challenged the look-out.

"It is I, Linz of the house of Clay!" announced Linz with as much confidence as he could muster. The head of the guards quickly approached when he heard that it was Linz that had arrived.

"This is an unexpected but timely visit," said the head of the guards respectfully. "Why do you cross the lake at night?"

"I am here to represent my uncle, the chief of this clan."

"I had planned to sail to Halawa myself in the morning to see your uncle," explained the head of the guards. "You see, the prisoners we are holding, they have just tried to escape, but we have managed to restrain them."

"Have they been harmed?"

"No, we have them tied up securely now, but they have bruised and battered a few of my men," said the head of the guards.

Linz jumped onto the dock, after attaching the boat securely. "Your men will heal," Linz remarked with little compassion. "My uncle has sent me to collect the prisoners and take them to Halawa. I will take them with me tonight."

"He has sent no men with you for protection?" the head guard asked in concern.

"The matter is too sensitive. No one must know of their presence here."

"Then I will travel with you, to help you escort the prisoners to Halawa," offered the head of the guards.

Linz was starting to get worried, and it showed. "That won't be necessary," he said quickly. "If they are tied securely then I will simply lie them in the bottom of the boat and sail them directly to my uncle's private mooring."

The head of the guards looked uncertain at this arrangement, but Linz was his uncle's heir, the chief of the Lake Men. It seemed unwise to argue.

"Right then. I'll get my men to load the prisoners into your boat."

"Give me their weapons too," instructed Linz. "My uncle wants to inspect them."

CHAPTER 37

Ganry was feeling angry with himself - angry that their plan had failed, angry that they had been unable to escape, angry that they had found themselves in this position to begin with. He was seething that his death was going to be so miserable and ignoble, executed like a common criminal, bound from head to toe with thick rope.

"Get up now, scum," snarled one of the guards, roughly yanking Ganry into a standing position.

"This is it," thought Ganry to himself, seeing that Artas, Hendon, and Barnaby were also being lifted to their feet.

"How are we going to do this?" asked one guard to another.

"Drag them?"

"Too awkward, isn't it?" countered the first. "Be easier if we carry them? One in each end?"

"Fair enough," nodded the second guard. "Alright boys!" he shouted to the group of guards milling around uncertainly. "Two men to each prisoner, one at the head and one at the feet. Take it slowly and make sure that those ropes stay tight!"

"They're going to feed us to the water dragons!" whispered Artas to Ganry, panic in his eyes. Ganry groaned inwardly, an even more pathetic way to die.

The soldiers clumsily hoisted the prisoners up and stumbled along the walkway. Ganry was expecting to hit the water at any moment.

"The boat is just at the end of this pier!" shouted one of the soldiers.

"Great, they're going to take us out into the middle of the lake to make sure that we have no chance of surviving," grumbled Ganry to himself, resigned to the fate of a watery death.

"Right, throw them in," shouted the guard. "Make sure that they're all nice and flat down on the bottom of the boat."

"Ungh!" grunted Ganry, landing heavily as he was unceremoniously chucked onto the wooden craft. One by one, each of the prisoners were thrown on board, tumbling on top of each other, crunching and bruising as each of them landed heavily on the other. Eventually Ganry could feel the boat pushing away from the pier, beginning to bob gently across the lake. Ganry closed his eyes and tried to be thankful for the few small pleasures that his life had brought him.

As soon as the boat was out of sight of the fishing outpost, Linz dropped the sail and brought it to almost a standstill, far out in the middle of the lake. He pulled a small dagger from his belt and began to cut the ties of the prisoners that had been thrown into the bottom of the boat.

Lying on top was Barnaby, and with a few quick slices of his blade Linz began to pull the ropes from Barnaby's ankles and wrists, helping the small elderly man unsteadily to his feet and across the boat to one of the small wooden benches that lined the side. Next was Hendon. Linz worked quickly to cut through the ropes, pulling Hendon up off the others beneath him. Next to be freed was Artas. Linz's blade slicing cleanly through the ropes that firmly bound him. Once Artas was free, Linz turned his attention to Ganry.

"What the hell is going on!" muttered Ganry, surprised and confused at having the ropes cut from him at a moment when he had been expecting to meet his death in the cold dark waters of the deep lake.

"Quickly! You have to stand up, move out of the way!" urged Linz.

"Hmmph," came a muffled moan from beneath Ganry.

"Princess, are you okay?" asked Linz with concern in his voice.

As Linz helped to lift Ganry up from the bottom of the boat, Myriam began to struggle out from beneath the cloaks that had been concealing her.

"You heavy oafs!" exclaimed Myriam angrily. "You nearly killed me! I thought I was going to suffocate with all of you lying on top of me like sacks of potatoes!"

"What were doing down there?" asked Ganry, flabbergasted at the turn of events. "Who is this? What's going on?" He gestured towards Linz.

"Calm down, Ganry." Myriam dusted herself off. "We're rescuing you."

"You're rescuing us?" asked Ganry in disbelief. "We're supposed to be protecting you!"

"Well, you're not doing a very good job of it!" laughed Myriam. "Besides, you're being very rude. None of you have thanked Linz here for his incredible bravery in helping you to escape from certain death."

"My apologies," said Ganry, turning to Linz. "Thank you. But I'm afraid I'm still not sure who you are?"

"Linz is the heir to the clan of the lake men," explained Myriam. "His uncle, the chief of the clan, had decided that we would be a perfect match to be married, an idea that neither of us was particularly thrilled about, so I persuaded Linz to help me rescue you." Linz seemed embarrassed with all of the attention and the praise being heaped on him.

Ganry addressed Myriam. "So what's the plan now then, Princess? Now that you've rescued us so bravely?"

"Um, I hadn't really got that far to be honest," admitted Myriam.

"You will have to sail this boat across the lake until you come to the Temple Stream." Linz pointed into the distance. "That's the only stream that flows out of the lake. It will take you to the north. It is the only way that you will be able to reach a trail that will take you to the outside world."

"You're coming with us, aren't you?" asked Artas hopefully, intrigued by the young lake boy.

Linz shook his head regretfully. "No, I have to return to my people."

"Won't your uncle be angry with you?" Myriam was concerned for the safety of her new-found friend.

"I will tell them that you overpowered me," said Linz, thinking quickly. "Perhaps if you cut me or beat me, it will look more believable. Then I will swim back to Halawa from here."

"You can't swim from here!" insisted Myriam. "It's too far! And what about the water dragons? It's not safe for you, Linz."

"I am a strong swimmer. Don't worry. The water dragons generally hunt near the shore, it would be rare for them to be looking for prey in deep water. I will be safe. I need to look like I have been attacked though. Can one of you hit me hit me in the face?"

None of them were eager to hit someone who had just moments ago rescued them from likely death.

"Come on, punch me!"

"Fine, I'll do it," said Artas, stepping forward. Linz braced himself for the impact of the blow.

"Ow!" grunted Linz, as Artas slapped the back of his hand across Linz's cheek.

Ganry shook his head. "No, you'll need to do it harder than that, Artas. That's barely made his cheek blush. You're going to need to draw blood. Do you want me to do it?"

"No, I can do it," insisted Artas. He drew his arm back and brought the back of his hand fiercely against Linz's face.

"Aagh!" howled Linz, feeling the pain of the blow.

"Again!" instructed Ganry. "Try and bruise the eye." Artas forcefully slapped Linz again. "And once more," insisted Ganry, "this time try and cut the lip." Artas hit

Linz across the face again, the power of the blow knocked Linz to the floor of the boat.

"This seems an awful way to be thanking you for rescuing us," protested Myriam, helping Linz back to his feet.

"It's what needs to be done. Now cut me."

"What?" asked Artas. "What do you mean cut you?"

"Use your knife, slash me across the chest. Just enough to damage my tunic and cut my skin, draw some blood. It will look more realistic."

"If you're sure," Artas said uncertainly, collecting his knife from the bundle of weapons that Linz had liberated from the fishing outpost. He weighed the knife carefully in his hand, and then delicately used the blade to cut several slashes in the tunic that Linz was wearing.

"Cut *me*," reiterated Linz, pulling apart his tunic and exposing his smooth, hairless chest. Artas placed the sharp edge of his dagger's blade against Linz's skin and dragged it slowly across his chest, drawing a line of bright crimson blood as the blade sliced over where the young boy's heart would be.

"Very good, you look sufficiently beaten up now," grinned Ganry. "Like a gang of mountain thieves have taken everything you own."

"Thank you," said Myriam, gently kissing Linz on the cheek. Linz winced with pain as her lips brushed his bruised face.

"I have no way to thank you," said Artas gravely.

"I'll remember you by the scars on my skin," smiled Linz, placing his hand on Artas's shoulder, before slipping over the side of the boat and into the dark water below.

Myriam watched Linz swimming quietly away into the distance.

CHAPTER 38

"Please sir, I cannot sign this, it is unconstitutional," begged Judge Strogen, the Chief Judge of the Kingdom of Palara.

"Sign it!" screamed Duke Harald, incensed with fury.

"But you cannot be King while there lives a rightful heir with a stronger claim than you," said the judge feebly.

"I know that you fool, but this will at least bring me one step closer. Sign it!" Harald slammed the wooden table with his fist.

They were in the throne room of Castle Villeroy. Harald was sitting at a plain wooden table, within touching distance of the throne that he coveted so fiercely.

"If you kill the King," began the judge.

"The question is not *if*," interrupted Harald. "Sign that bit of paper and my fool of a brother will meet his death at sunrise! I will rule the Kingdom as Regent until we have been able to find that witch of girl Myriam, and bring her back to Villeroy in chains."

"In all good conscious, sir," protested the judge, "it would go against everything that I have sought to uphold. It would go against all the ancient laws of this land. It would leave me with no integrity and I would be bringing the office of Chief Judge into disrepute. I cannot sign that death warrant."

"Then I shall find a new Chief Judge who will!" hissed Harald, quickly drawing his short dagger and slitting the throat of the elderly man who cowered before him.

Harald wiped the blood from the blade of his dagger on the black robes of the dead man who lay at his feet. He calmly walked around the table and resumed his seat, turning towards him the parchment on which was written the death warrant of his brother. Harald picked up the elaborate quill, carefully dipped it in the small pot of ink that stood nearby, and slowly and deliberately signed the name of Chief Judge Strogen.

CHAPTER 39

King Ludwig squinted into the morning sun as it rose to the east of the castle. It had been a long time since he had been outside in the fresh morning air, away from the dungeon in which his brother had imprisoned him. Somehow, he cherished the sunrise even more, knowing that it would be the last that he would see.

The muted rhythm of the single drummer began to beat, the death march always played before an execution. The courtyard that they were in was known as the Judge's Courtyard because it was reserved for punishments and executions overseen by the judges of the Kingdom of Palara. King Ludwig could feel his wife Alissia shivering beside him. He reached out and took her hand, their fingers entwining as he tried to offer some small comfort to her, on the last day that they would spend together. They were surrounded by soldiers, but somehow it felt as if they were alone in the world, together, watching the sun slowly rise in the east.

Duke Harald entered the courtyard from a wooden door with two sentries posted either side. It was the door that led directly to the throne room. Harald sat himself down on the wooden chair from which King Ludwig would normally observe proceedings such as these. The Duke's gaze was steely, ice-cold, his face displayed no emotion. The King was surprised not to see Judge Strogen, the Chief Judge. A death warrant of this magnitude would require his signature and his authority. King Ludwig looked across the courtyard to where the blood-stained block of wood stood. A shiver ran down his spine.

Normally the Chief Judge would read out the death warrant and confirm the sentence, but today the only sound was the steady drum.

Zaim, Duke Harald's arms-bearer, motioned to the guards. They took hold of King Ludwig's arms and walked him into the middle of the courtyard towards the executioner's block. The executioner in his black hood stood beside the wooden block, patiently resting his large axe on the stones beneath his feet. The King knelt down on the cold stones, and placed his neck in the purpose-built groove that was carved in the wooden block.

A druid stepped forward from beside Duke Harald and chanted a short invocation. The soldiers stood to one side and the executioner moved into position, slowly lifting his iron axe and then bringing it swiftly down, the blade slicing cleanly through King Ludwig's neck, ending his reign as the ruler of the Kingdom of Palara.

Queen Alissia gasped in horror as the axe blade fell and ended the life of her husband. She closed her eyes so that she didn't have to watch the executioner pick up her husband's lifeless head, his body dragged unceremoniously away. She heard the splash of water as the executioner tipped a bucket of hot water over the wooden block, washing away the blood that had been spilled.

Queen Alissia opened her eyes as she felt the soldiers roughly grab her by the arms, walking her towards the center of the courtyard. The druid stepped forward once more and said a brief invocation before the death sentence was imposed on the Queen. The drum continued to beat steadily and slowly. Queen Alissia knelt down, feeling the cold hard stones of the courtyard beneath her. She felt numb, tired, beyond fear, as if these final moments of her life were part of some terrifying dream, a dream from which she couldn't awake.

The Queen placed her neck down on to the wooden block, feeling the warm wetness of the water with which it had just been cleaned. She closed her eyes, trying to block out everything that was happening around her, everything that had happened, everything that was about to happen. She did not see the executioner slowly raising his heavy iron axe. She did not hear its blade falling quickly towards her. She did not feel the pain as her life was violently ended.

"It is done," said Duke Harald, standing up from his wooden chair and beginning to walk from the courtyard.

"What should we do with the bodies?" asked Zaim. "Will there be a funeral for your brother and his wife?"

"A funeral?" repeated Harald, contemplating the idea. "No. No funeral. They are traitors to the Kingdom of Palara. Mount their heads on spikes and display them at the castle gate. Let their deaths be a warming to all other traitors that may be sympathizers of my brother or his wretched daughter. There will be no mercy for traitors. There will be no honor for traitors. There will be no funerals for traitors." Harald turned and left the courtyard, returning to the throne room.

Alone, Harald took off his cloak and sat on the golden throne reserved for the ruler of the Kingdom. Regent of the Kingdom did not have the same satisfying ring that being King would have, but until Princess Myriam was found and killed, then Regent was all that he could be. Slowly but surely, Duke Harald was edging towards the fulfillment of his dreams.

CHAPTER 40

The Duchess was sitting in her study having an early breakfast, enjoying the warmth of the sunrise as the rays from the east began to brighten the room. Breakfast was one of the Duchess's favorite meals of the day. Today she had ordered poached hens eggs and toasted muffins. She smiled contentedly to herself as she sliced through one of the eggs, releasing its soft yellow yolk to flood gently over the crumpet.

"Excuse me, Your Excellence?" politely interrupted one of her pages. "I'm sorry to disturb your breakfast, but you sent for your Captain of the Guard, Captain Versance?"

"Of course, send him in."

"Your Excellence," bowed Captain Versance, always a stickler for protocol.

"Come in, captain," gestured the Duchess.

"Are you sure you wouldn't prefer me to come back after you have finished your breakfast?"

"Nonsense, captain," dismissed the Duchess. "We have more important things to discuss than breakfast. Come, take a seat. Let me pour you some tea while you tell me about your progress in calling together our army."

"Well, as you have commanded, we have called all able bodied men to report to the Castle," began the captain, as the Duchess started to pour tea from her favorite delicate china tea pot. Suddenly, the Duchess's hand began to shake, and the tea pot began to wobble. "Your Excellence?" asked the captain, concerned by the Duchess's shakiness. The Duchess continued to struggle to control the teapot, tea spilling messily over the table in front of her. "Your Excellence? Your Excellence? Are you okay?" The Duchess seemed to have a glazed look over her face. Suddenly the teapot fell from her hand, rolling across the table and falling onto the stone floor where it smashed into a multitude of pieces. The Duchess slumped back in her chair, not responding to the captain's concerned queries.

"Aaaaggghh!" screamed the Duchess, her body wracked with pain as she slid down onto the floor.

"Your Excellence!" shouted the captain, leaping to his feet. "Raise the alarm! Raise the alarm! The Duchess has fallen ill!" Maids and pages quickly dashed into the room, helping the captain to lift the Duchess to her feet. "Take her to her bedroom!" instructed the captain. "Call the doctors! Call the doctors!"

"My daughter," sobbed the Duchess suddenly. "My daughter. Oh my dear daughter, I'm so sorry."

"Your Excellence? Your Excellence? What is it? What's the matter? What is it that pains you?"

"My daughter... my daughter is dead," sobbed the Duchess. "He has killed her. He has killed them both."

"Who has? Duke Harald?"

"He's executed them. I watched them die."

"Your Excellence, please just rest now, the doctors will be here soon. They will give you something to help you relax," comforted the captain.

"No!" shouted the Duchess, sitting up suddenly from her bed, her voice becoming steely and firm. "No. I have no need of doctors. We have wasted too much time already. Call my army together! I will rain fire down on that mad man! I will not rest until I tear him limb from limb! I will feed his eyes to the crows and scatter his ashes to the wind so that his name will be forgotten for all time!" The captain had never seen the Duchess so enraged, her fury was terrifying, all-consuming, filling the room with her anger and anguish. "Go now, captain!" instructed the Duchess darkly. "Go now. We both have a lot of work to do."

The captain bowed deeply as he left the room.

CHAPTER 41

"I feel sick," said Myriam, suddenly clutching the side of the boat.

Artas rushed to her side. "What is it, Princess? What's the matter?"

"I... I don't know," gasped Myriam, clutching her stomach. "I just feel blackness, everywhere blackness."

"I feel it too," nodded Hendon. "Something has taken the light. There is something evil, something powerful."

"What are you both talking about?" Ganry continued to steer the boat. "I don't feel anything. Barnaby, you take care of Myriam and Hendon. Artas, help me point the boat towards the Temple Stream. We've got to get off this lake as quickly as possible."

Artas moved over to give Ganry a hand. "We're getting closer to the shore. Do we know what a water dragon looks like?"

"I'm sure we'll know one if we see one. Let's just take it steady. The Temple Stream must be just up ahead. Barnaby, how are those two doing?"

"Cold, but calmer. It's almost as if they're falling into some sort of sleep. Will we be able to find somewhere to rest tonight?"

"I'm inclined to stay on the boat to be honest. We need to put some distance between us and those lake men."

"Wait, what's that?" Artas leaned over the side of the boat, looking down into the water. "I saw something move down there."

"Stay calm, stay calm," soothed Ganry. "No need to panic until we know what we're dealing with."

"Whoah!" Artas jumped as the boat lurched suddenly.

"That wasn't good." Ganry drew his sword Wind-Storm from its scabbard.

"I think we've found a water dragon."

"Or a water dragon has found us. Stay back from the edge of the boat, it might decide that we're too big to worry about if we don't provoke it."

Artas grunted as he fell against the mast, knocked off balance as the boat lurched again, as if it was being pushed to one side or run aground on some rocks.

"I think that's just it's tail hitting us," said Ganry. "Maybe trying to tip us over. If we can get a look at its head, I'll take a swing at it."

"Watch out!" yelled Artas, as the craft lurched again.

Ganry crouched at one end of the boat, sword at the ready. "Can you see its shape?"

"It seems long long and thin." Artas tried to catch a glimpse of whatever it was that that was buffeting their boat. "Maybe a bit like a snake? A big snake?"

"A snake? I hate snakes! Why does it have to be a snake?"

"There! There's it's head!" pointed Artas.

"It's too dark, I can't see anything. Careful!" The boat lurched once more as the water dragon bumped it again with its tail.

"Don't antagonize it," cautioned Barnaby.

"Antagonize it?" asked Ganry incredulously. "It attacked us, remember?"

Barnaby shook his head, while clutching the side of the boat. "It's just a wild animal. We've entered its territory. The more that we act like prey, the more it will hunt us."

"So what would you suggest?"

"There's the temple that we've been looking for." A dark building slowly emerged from the mist. "That's the beginning of the Temple Stream. Pull up there, stop the boat there."

"Really? You want to stop the boat while we are being stalked by a water dragon?" asked Ganry in disbelief.

"Yes! That's exactly why we need to stop the boat."

"There's a pier outside the temple," indicated Artas. "Can you guide us in there?"

"If our watery friend doesn't tip us over first," said Ganry, rolling his eyes. "Take the rope, Artas. You'll need to jump to the pier to pull us in tight and secure the mooring. Ready? One... Two... Now!"

Artas leaped across the small gap between the bobbing boat and the small wooden pier that extended from the temple, quickly wrapping the rope around one of the mooring posts to secure it.

"I can't see the snake!" shouted Artas.

"Don't call it a snake," growled Ganry. "Let's call it a water dragon. Somehow that makes me feel better."

"There it is!" Artas peered at the long dark shape, moving gracefully under the water. "It's still circling us!"

Barnaby watched it swimming lazily around them. "Relax. Let's just get everyone off the boat and into the temple."

Artas was still worried. "Can they not climb on to land?"

"We know nothing about these beasts. We just need to tread carefully."

Artas and Ganry helped Barnaby to lift Myriam and and Hendon out of the boat.

"Artas, go with Barnaby." Ganry stood as far away from the edge of the pier as possible. "See what that temple holds for us and whether we can bunker down here for the night. I'll try and keep an eye on what this water dragon is up to."

With his dagger drawn, Artas led the way off the pier. They headed towards the temple, which appeared to be built on stilts over the water in the style of the lake men.

"It looks deserted," said Artas quietly, feeling his way through the darkness. "This door is open." He pushed cautiously against the large wooden door that seemed to give access to the temple buildings.

"What have you found?" whispered Ganry, coming up behind the group, sword still drawn, warily peering into the darkness around them.

"Deserted I think. Any sign of that water dragon?"

"No, it seems to have lost interest once we stopped moving. Barnaby was right."

"We should probably try and spend the night here," pondered Artas. "If we could just get a fire or something going, we'll be able to see what we're dealing with."

"Maybe I can help you with that," said a voice from deep within the darkness.

Ganry moved protectively in front of the the others. "Who's there?" he challenged.

A small light flickered at the rear of the temple.

"My name is Ghaffar. Welcome to my temple. I've been expecting you."

CHAPTER 42

"Quickly Arexos, quickly!" urged Badr al Din. "The master Qutaybah arrives today. Everything must be perfect or it will be me that will be sent to the slave market."

Areas did his best to carry the enormous platters of fruit through to the quarters that would be used by Qutaybah, the master of Villa Salamah, to which Arexos now belonged.

Arexos's days of living in the Kingdom of Palara seemed a long time ago, a different lifetime almost. His life had taken an unexpected turn when he, and his master Hendrickson, had been betrayed by the Narc smugglers and sold into slavery. Arexos often wondered what had become of Henrickson. He hoped that he was safe and well somewhere.

In the early days of his captivity, Arexos had dreamed that Henrickson would come and rescue him. He imagined that Henrickson would turn up out of the blue one day, storming in, shouting his name, searching for Arexos. But as the days had dragged on into weeks, that fantasy faded. He became resigned to his day-to-day reality of life as a slave at Villa Salamah, under the direction of Badr al Din, the chief housekeeper of the villa.

"Sir, what's he like?" asked Arexos, working alongside Bard al Din. They were changing the cushion covers that covered the floor of Qutaybah's sleeping quarters.

"Who?" replied Badr al Din impatiently, focused on the task at hand.

"The master Qutaybah. The man that we belong to. I was just wondering, what's he like?" repeated Arexos.

"You are always so full of questions!" laughed Badr al Din. "It is unlikely that you will meet him, he's a very private man. He likes things done perfectly, no surprises."

"How will he travel, when he arrives here today?"

"Well, of course he will ride his horse, like all nobles do."

"But will he travel alone, or will he have servants with him? Or family?" persisted Arexos.

"He doesn't have family. Villa Salamah was part of the estate of the master's father. Qutaybah inherited everything when his father died. He may travel with a small number of slaves, but generally he just travels with his security guards. They are hired soldiers that answer to him alone. Some people call them the assassins."

"What do you mean? The assassins?"

"That's enough!" snapped Badr al Din. "I've said too much already. The master does not tolerate idle gossip."

Arexos felt a little nervous but also excited at the prospect of meeting the powerful man who held Arexos' life in his hands.

A distant bell was echoed by a bell rung in the grounds of the villa.

"That's the signal!" gasped Badr al Din in alarm. "They are coming. The watch-tower has alerted us. Qutaybah is coming! Quickly now, let me make a final check... good yes, good, I think we are ready. Go now, back to your quarters until I call for you!"

Arexos almost did as he was told, retreating out of sight of the main building of the villa compound, but he didn't go and conceal himself within the slaves' rooms as Badr al Din had instructed. Arexos was curious and wanted to catch a glimpse of Qutaybah. He had never seen a Vandemland noble before, and he wondered how they differed from the nobles of the Kingdom of Palara.

Arexos didn't have long to wait. In just a few moments he could hear the clattering of horses hooves across the stones and pebbles that lined the forecourt. Peering discretely around a corner, he could see the boys from the stables come running to take care of the horses of Qutaybah and his men. Arexos saw Badr al Din walking out to meet the party.

"Master! Welcome to your home!" exclaimed Badr al Din formally, bowing deeply and respectfully. A large man walked past Badr al Din, seeming to not even acknowledge his existence. It was clear to Arexos that this was Qutaybah. He walked with power and with purpose. Arexos only caught a brief glimpse of him. A tall man, broad shoulders, his ebony skin contrasting sharply with the white robes that he wore. Arexos wondered what language he spoke, what it would be like to serve such a man, and how different it would be serving Qutaybah compared to serving Henrickson.

Arexos began to wander slowly back towards the slaves' quarters, assuming Qutaybah would be secluded within his quarters for the rest of the day. As Arexos was trailing his fingers through the cool trickling water of one of the fountains that lined the courtyard, he was surprised by a deep voice from behind him.

"Who are you?" It was a voice that Arexos didn't recognize, its suddenness startled him. He turned slowly and was intimidated to realize that it was Qutaybah himself who stood behind him, watching him carefully. Before Arexos could speak, Badr al Din bustled forward, bowing deeply.

"I'm so sorry master, so sorry. It is just a new slave that we have been training, no need to concern yourself with him. He was just on his way back to the slaves' quarters," groveled Badr al Din.

"No, he wasn't," contradicted Qutaybah firmly. He wasn't going anywhere. "This boy isn't used to being a slave. Where did you find him?"

"He was purchased from the slave market," explained Badr al Din.

"Where are you from, boy?" demanded Qutaybah, addressing Arexos.

"He's from..." began Badr al Din, trying to retain some sort of control over the situation.

"I asked the boy!" snapped Qutaybah, quickly silencing the housekeeper. "Answer me boy, where are you from?"

Arexos was unsure of the protocol for addressing a man such as Qutaybah. "I'm from the Kingdom of Palara... your... royalness."

"Palara?" noted Qutaybah with interest. "Badr al Din, you should know better than to buy slaves from Palara. But anyway, assign the boy to my quarters. He will attend to my needs during my stay."

"Master please," began Badr al Din, "the boy is only new, let me offer you a more experienced..."

"Enough with your sniveling!" snapped Qutaybah. "My orders are clear. Do not give me an excuse to cut your head off."

Badr al Din bowed as low as possible, his forehead pressed to the ground beneath him. "Yes, master."

Arexos looked at Qutaybah in awe, there was something incredibly compelling and magnetic about this man.

"You haven't learned how to bow yet boy?" asked Qutaybah, raising an querying eyebrow towards Arexos. Arexos hurriedly attempted a bow, so clumsy that it drew a good-natured laugh from Qutaybah. "Come," he smiled, "it's been a long journey. Draw me a bath. Hopefully you are better at that than you are at bowing."

CHAPTER 43

"All rise for the Regent of Palara!" boomed the loud voice of the footman, announcing the arrival of Duke Harald into the throne room. Harald carefully sat on the great throne, knowing that it would cause grumblings among the conservative members of the nobility, but not caring anymore about whose sensitivities were trampled, or whose egos were bruised.

This was an important moment. He had called the heads of all the noble families of the kingdom together. His first official act since declaring himself Regent of Palara.

The room had fallen silent as soon as he had entered, and he let that pregnant pause hang over the assembled gathering. He liked the sense of anticipation, that they were hanging on his every breath, waiting for his words of wisdom.

"My Lords and Ladies," began Harald eventually, choosing his words carefully. "I have called you together to warn of a dire threat against against us all, a dire threat against our very Kingdom." Harald slowly looked around the room. He already knew who his allies were, and which of the noble families remained loyal to his brother, or at least the memory of the dead King. He would deal with those sympathizers later, quietly. This was a moment for leadership, not for retribution.

"The events of past few weeks have been upsetting for us all. My own family has been torn apart by betrayal, mistrust, and treason. But for the good of our kingdom we cannot dwell on the past. With the death of my brother King Ludwig, the rightful heir to the throne is my niece, the Princess Myriam. Unfortunately, Myriam has been abducted from the castle, and we believe that she is being held by brigands in the Cefinon Forest. We hope and pray to the gods that she remains safe, but we fear that she may have already met a violent death. All of our efforts are focused on finding Myriam and returning her to her rightful place on the throne of our beloved Kingdom. In the meantime, I have agreed to accept the heavy responsibility of ruling as Regent, merely to ensure that there is some stability and leadership for our country during this difficult time."

Duke Harald paused and looked around the assembled throng of nobles, trying to gauge how much resistance he would face. He would kill them all if he had to. He had come too far now. What was one more life? Ten more lives? One hundred more lives? The druids had foretold that he could be King, he simply had to make it happen.

"My Lords and Ladies of Palara, while we have had our problems, our threats do not come from within the

Kingdom, they lie on our borders. We have received intelligence that the barbarians of Vandemland have been building their forces, readying themselves for an attack on our beloved kingdom." Harald paused for effect at this point. He was pleased to see worry and concern cross the faces of the nobles. It had been a long time since Palara had been threatened by war, a long time since the Kingdom had been embroiled in any sort of major conflict.

"Our homes, our families, our very way of life is under threat," continued Harald. "We must mobilize our army at once. We must prepare our fleet for battle. We must take the initiative and destroy our enemies before they have an opportunity to inflict any damage on us." There were nods and murmurs of approval. Harald smiled, he knew that he had them where he wanted them.

"Of course, wars of any kind are expensive. It will take all of our reserves to equip our army and build the ships necessary in order to launch a major offensive against the barbarians of Vandemland. Each of us must play our part. Each of us must make sacrifices in order for our campaign to be successful, and in order for us to be victorious. For this reason, I am imposing a twenty per cent tax on all households. Twenty per cent of the value of each estate will be forfeited to the crown of Palara for the purposes of funding our defense."

There was an audible gasp from around the room as the assembled nobles began to register what Harald had just said. A twenty per cent tax was crippling, especially as it would be charged on top of the existing range of taxes that were already being collected. For many it would mean that they would have to sell significant parts of their property, or forfeit them to the crown in lieu of payment of taxes - a consequence that Harald was not unhappy about at all.

With his speech concluded, Harald stood and waited patiently while the assembled nobles slowly realized that they were expected to bow and curtsy to the Regent, who was now their ruler. Harald made a silent note of those who were slow to bow, slow to show their respect for him. They would be the first to feel his wrath, to feel the power of the new order in the Kingdom of Palara.

CHAPTER 44

"I've got someone here who has been searching for you." Ghaffar stoked the fire before him, illuminating the room with its flickering flames.

"What do you mean?" Ganry demanded.

Ghaffar looked over the group, his eyes finally settling on Myriam. "Well, to be precise, I have someone here who is searching for *her*."

Ganry was ready to pounce at the first sign of hostility. "How do you know who we are?"

"There are no secrets from the trees," shrugged Ghaffar mysteriously.

"Ganry," said Myriam softly, beginning to recover from the darkness that she had felt on the boat. "I think we can trust this monk. I feel quite safe here."

"I agree," Barnaby added.

Ganry was not appeased in the slightest. "Who is waiting here? Where are they?" he growled at the monk.

"Calm yourself, friend. Don't be scared. Come with me. The main temple buildings are away from the water, and they are waiting for you there."

Ganry was uncertain of what exactly was happening, but Myriam seemed determined to trust the monk. Ganry followed warily with his sword drawn, as Ghaffar moved quickly through the back of the temple room, and out into a complex of buildings surrounded by the trees of the forest.

"Princess Myriam, may I present to you Zander Moncrieff and his men, Aban, Yasir, Najid, and Karam," announced Ghaffar formally.

"Princess," said Zander respectfully as he and his men knelt and bowed. "It is a great relief to finally find you safe and well."

"You have been searching for me?" Myriam asked uncertainly.

Ganry stood protectively in front of Myriam, pointing his sword at the men. "Who are you? Who sent you?"

Zander motioned at his men to remain at ease. He directed his words at Myriam, ignoring Ganry's hostility and drawn blade. "Princess, we are from the Berghein Valley. We have been sent by the Duchess D'Anjou. The Duchess has sent us to find you and return you to the safety of her protection at Castle Locke."

"My grandmother? My grandmother sent you?" gasped Myriam. "You are from Castle Locke?"

"How do we know that this isn't some kind of trick?" growled Ganry. "Duke Harald has his best hunters searching for Myriam, how do we know that you are who you say you are?"

"The Duchess foresaw that you may be cautious. She entrusted me with her dagger. It carries the same stones as the ring of Locke that Myriam wears. The stones grow brighter when they are brought together." Zander slowly pulled the dagger out from the leather sheath that he wore on his belt, holding Ganry's stern gaze to show that he meant no harm. The dagger that the Duchess had entrusted him with was a small weapon. It looked almost inconsequential, perhaps decorative, but the stonework and engraving on it was exquisite.

A small sigh of recognition escaped from between Myriam's lips as she gazed at the blade. She raised her left hand and the assembled men could see the ring there. As she reached out towards the dagger that Zander held, the stones began to glow brighter, both the stones inlaid on the ring and the stones set on the dagger hilt.

"This is wonderful," laughed Myriam. "Let me introduce my companions, my friends. My protector is Ganry de Rosenthorn, my fearless archer is Artas of the House of Holstein, our wise and learned friend is Barnaby, and this helpful young man is Hendon."

"I am pleased that you have been in good company my Princess," bowed Zander. "The Duchess will be keen to thank and honor each of you personally as soon as we reach the safety of Castle Locke."

Ganry slid WindStorm back into it's scabbard. "How easy will it be to reach Castle Locke from here?" he asked, unsure really where in the forest that they were.

"Well, we may need some guidance from our friendly monk Ghaffar here, but we're not too far from the border between Palara and the Berghein Valley, so we will just need to find a way to avoid their border controls and we will back amidst the safety of our own people."

"We will need to move quickly then. We have the lake men on our heels and Duke Harald's men scouring the roads for any sign of us."

"Yes, you will need to leave just as dawn begins to break," agreed Ghaffar. "The lake men won't sail in the dark, but they will guess that you will have attempted to flee in this direction. So they will be paddling in their boats as soon as the sun rises."

"Can you show us the way back to the road, Ghaffar?" asked Zander.

"Yes, but how will you travel?"

"He has a point," said Ganry. "We had to leave our horses behind with the lake men." Ganry was upset that he had to leave his beloved horse, Bluebell, behind. They had been through a lot. It was odd to think that their journey together had ended so abruptly.

"We will have to ride two to a horse," suggested Zander practically. "We can sort out the logistics in the morning. We don't have any other option. We'll need to travel as quickly as possible in order to try and avoid detection."

"I have a question," said Ganry suddenly. "The water dragons, what do they look like?"

"Well," began Ghaffar thoughtfully, "they have a long body and tail, and they move through the water like a snake. I guess you could just describe them as a very big snake."

"Thank you," frowned Ganry. "You have no idea how unhappy that makes me."

CHAPTER 45

"Myriam grows stronger," said the druid, peering into the smoke that rose from the bowl, which he swirled over the flames of the flickering fire. The elderly druid sat on the floor of the temple, and opposite sat Duke Harald, Regent of the Kingdom of Palara.

"Stronger?" questioned Harald. "What do you mean, stronger? How can she be growing stronger?! She is a girl hiding amidst the trees of the Cefinon Forest!" The Duke's eyes were red from the smoke, his words hissed from between his teeth, a vein throbbed alarmingly in his right temple.

"The stones are drawing together... the stones of the Berghein Valley," continued the druid, studying the smoke.

"Berghein," snarled the Duke, "I knew that old witch was not to be trusted. What are these stones that you speak of?"

The druid breathed deeply, surrounded by the pungent smoke that filled the temple, staining the walls as they had been stained for centuries. The relationship of the druids to the rulers of Palara was a complicated one. While they recognized no one as their master, they had been used as trusted advisers to the powerful since the days of the great chief Terrick. The druids had been at his side then, and they still sat at the side of the House of Villeroy.

"The Berghein Stones are old, ancient stones, powerful stones... their coming together symbolizes the uniting of a family... uniting against you, my Duke," whispered the druid.

"Ha! You and your stupid old prophecies," dismissed Harald contemptuously. "There is no power in stones! There is only power in weapons - in steel and in iron, weapons that will destroy any family that dares to stand against me. Weapons that will destroy the armies of the Duchess D'Anjou and her wretched brood from the Berghein Valley." Duke Harald stood impatiently and began pacing the room. "Tell me... tell me of my victory... tell me when I will be crowned King of Palara!"

"I can only see what the smoke will reveal to me."

"You old fool," sneered the Prince. "You're all fools. I should cut off your head and burn this place to the ground!"

"My death would be inconsequential, as has been my life," replied the druid calmly.

"Why won't you tell me what I want to hear!" shouted Harald, his voice echoing around the small temple.

"Perhaps you are not listening to what I am telling you," suggested the druid.

"What do mean?"

"There is a power in the Berghein Valley that is drawing the ancient stones together. There is a family that is united against you. Perhaps Princess Myriam is just a distraction - your real threat lies within Castle Locke... your real threat is the power that is calling these stones home." The druid watched carefully as Harald tried to put the pieces of the puzzle together.

"So.... if I could strike at Castle Locke... if I could destroy the Duchess D'Anjou... Princess Myriam would have nowhere to turn, and I would soon rule not only the Kingdom of Palara but also all of the Berghein Valley as well!"

"Only the gods can see the future. We can but try and interpret the signs that they reveal to us."

"Druid, your life is spared for another day," growled Duke Harald. "My horse! Bring me my horse. I must return to Castle Villeroy. We have a battle to fight!"

Harald rode back to the castle as fast as his horse Thawban could carry him.

"A change of plan, Zaim!" announced the Duke, as his arms-bearer entered the throne room. Duke Harald was peering over a map of the region. "Vandemland is no longer our main problem. Instead we march on the Berghein Valley."

"The Berghein Valley, sir?" asked Zaim in surprise. "But Castle Locke is impregnable, it has never fallen. Do you intend to lay siege?"

"I intend to smash that miserable place to pieces... to dismantle it brick by brick... to erase it from the memory of time," snarled Harld, smashing his fist against the table.

"The fleet of ships that we have been preparing for the attack on Vandemland will be no use to us against the Berghein Valley," pointed out Zaim.

"We have not forgotten about Vandemland. Our ships will not be wasted, but if we are to realize our ambitions, it is Castle Locke that must fall first. It is the Duchess D'Anjou that must feel my wrath!"

"Understood, sir. We should be cautious not to underestimate the Berghein Valley. Do we have any information as to how large a force the Duchess has at her command?"

"We will send everything that we have. Let the full force of the armies of Palara rain down on her!"

"But the walls of Castle Locke," counseled Zaim. "We need some sort of strategy as to how we will break them."

"I have a strategy," grinned the Prince. "The druids have stores of fire-powder. We will line the walls of the castle with barrels of fire-powder and blow that old witch into the sky."

"But the druids only use the fire-powder in their ceremonies. They would never give it to us, especially if they knew that we planned to use it in battle?"

"The druids do not rule Palara, I do! Take a force of men and storm the druid's temple. Seize as many barrels of fire-powder that you can find."

"And if they resist, sir?"

"Of course they will resist," replied the Duke. "Slay them. Slay them all!"

CHAPTER 46

"Massage my shoulders, boy," instructed Qutaybah as Arexos helped to bathe his master. Villa Salamah wasn't his master's principal residence, but in the eyes of Arexos it was lavish. Qutaybah's private quarters at the villa contained a large bathing complex with a steam room, a dry sauna, and several different pools containing water heated to varying temperatures. Arexos poured some oil into the palms of his hands and began to gently apply it to the muscular shoulders of his master. He marveled at the contrast between the dark black skin of Qutaybah and his own white hands.

"Excuse me, master," interrupted the housekeeper Badr al Din, bowing as he cautiously entered the room.

"What is it?" snapped Qutaybah, annoyed at having his bath interrupted.

"I'm sorry sir, but your deputy has requested an audience with you." Badr al Din was still bowing deeply.

"Yazid? Of course, send him in."

"Would you like me to leave, master?" suggested Arexos.

"Of course not boy, keep massaging my shoulders, concentrate around the back of my neck, that's where the tension is."

"Sir," greeted Yazid, kneeling down on one knee and using his right hand to clasp his left wrist in front of his face in the traditional military greeting of Vandemland.

"What is it, Yazid? It must be important to be interrupting my bath?"

"I'm sorry sir, it is indeed important. I felt that you would want to hear this straight away. We have received a messenger from the Duchess D'Anjou of Castle Locke."

"The Duchess? Contacting us? That is unusual." Qutaybah became noticeably more interested in the conversation. "What does that old witch want?"

"She wants to employ us."

"She has a job for us?" laughed Qutaybah. "We are not some petty mercenaries for hire! We are the best soldiers that Vandemland has ever seen!"

"She is gathering her forces for an assault against the Kingdom of Palara. She plans to march against Duke Harald. She seeks our support, and she's happy to pay for it."

"Keep massaging my shoulders, boy."

Arexos hadn't realized that he had stopped. When he had heard mention of the Kingdom of Palara his mind had suddenly gone blank - it was the first time that he had thought of his homeland for days now. Arexos wondered what had happened to Henrickson, his master who he had traveled to Vandemland with, on the orders of Duke Harald, on the orders of the man against whom armies were gathering. At the urging of Qutaybah, Arexos quickly resumed massaging the big man's shoulders, trying to remain inconspicuous as the two soldiers continued their discussions.

"So if we were to accept the Duchess's commission, what would she have us do?" asked Qutaybah.

"She has asked that we travel to Castle Locke to meet with her there. She is gathering her forces in the Berghein Valley, and then plans to march on the Kingdom of Palara, pushing eastward until she has captured Castle Villeroy and slain Duke Harald."

"Fascinating," mused Qutaybah. "I'd always thought of the Duchess as being one of Palara's closest allies. However the coup by Duke Harald has obviously changed things."

"He has executed her daughter," advised Yazid, "and Myriam, who is the heir to the throne, is missing."

"Ah, I see," nodded Qutaybah. "There is nothing more dangerous than a mother who is forced to protect her children. I wonder if Duke Harald realized what trouble he was stirring up when he began to toy with the House of D'Anjou." Qutaybah closed his eyes as Arexos continued to steadily massage his muscles. Yazid remained standing silently beside the bath, waiting for some sort of instruction or indication from his leader as to what steps should be taken.

"What is our intelligence on the armies of the Kingdom of Palara?" asked Qutaybah, opening his eyes.

"Even well before the coup, Duke Harald had taken control of Palara's military," replied Yazid. "He significantly increased their ground forces and has also built a sizeable naval fleet. They are a formidable force. We had assumed that they were readying their forces for an attack against us here in Vandemland, but perhaps their focus has been the Berghein Valley all along."

"They do mean to attack you," interjected Arexos.

"Did I tell you to speak?" roared Qutaybah. "How dare you interrupt the conversation of your masters!"

"I'm sorry master, but Duke Harald does mean to launch an attack against Vandemland," insisted Arexos. "It's the reason that I am here... it's the reason that I was captured and sold as a slave."

"What are you talking about?" growled Qutaybah, turning to look intently at his young slave.

"Before I belonged to you I was a page to a man called Henrickson - he was the chief military adviser to Duke Harald of Palara," said Arexos quickly.

"Go on... I'm listening."

"Duke Harald sent Henrickson on a secret mission into Vandemland to assess the strengths and weaknesses, and to develop a plan of attack so that Palara could seize control of the territory. We paid a gang of Narc smugglers to get us across the border, but they betrayed us and sold us into slavery instead. I was bought by your household," finished Arexos.

"And Henrickson? What happened to him?" demanded Qutaybah.

"I'm not sure. I never saw him again."

Qutaybah nodded, a glimmer in his eye. He lay back in the bath and Arexos resumed massaging his broad muscular shoulders.

"You become more and more useful to me each day, boy," smiled Qutaybah. "So... the threat from Palara is real. I guess the question is, how do we respond? What sort of numbers can the Duchess muster against the armies of Palara?" asked Qutaybah, turning towards Yazid.

"She only has a small standing army. She has begun calling up the farmers and tradesmen of the Berghein Valley."

"Farmers and tradesmen," guffawed Qutaybah. "She is going to need more than farmers and tradesmen to take on Duke Harald!"

"I imagine that is why she has reached out to us," suggested Yazid.

"I imagine that is precisely why she has reached out to us," agreed Qutaybah. "But perhaps our interests have begun to align with the Duchess D'Anjou... an intriguing development. What I don't understand is why has she has approached us directly? She hasn't gone to the Caliphate of Vandemland to seek a formal alliance? She seeks to engage us as mercenaries? But then again, she may have done that, and the Caliphate is sensibly trying to keep some distance until this feud between his neighbors has played out. We have received no communication from the Caliphate on this?"

"Nothing, sir," confirmed Yazid. "Although the messenger from the Duchess asked specifically for you, and knew that you would be here at Villa Salamah."

"I see. Well, if we took our company of one hundred soldiers to the Berghein Valley and joined forces with the Duchess, it would certainly boost her fighting capability, but we would still be vastly outnumbered by the armies of the Kingdom of Palara. But then I can't believe that a woman as clever as the Duchess is planning to engage in a fight that she has no chance of winning. I imagine that she has a few tricks up her sleeve. She always does." Qutaybah closed his eyes. He appeared to be thinking, or sleeping. Arexos couldn't really tell.

"What are your orders, sir?" prompted Yazid.

"We will answer the call of the Duchess," replied Qutaybah firmly, opening his eyes suddenly and startling Arexos. "Gather our men. We will ride at sunrise. Let's see what Duke Harald has in store for us all."

CHAPTER 47

"Thank you, Ganry," said Myriam faintly, walking up behind the mercenary and placing a hand gently on his shoulder.

"Why are you thanking me?" Ganry continued to stare into the glowing embers of the fire that he had taken charge of lighting, as they had made camp for the evening. He knelt beside the fire, poking and prodding the logs that were now steadily burning.

"Because I would never have survived without you. I wouldn't have made it past that first night when Leonidavus smuggled me away from the castle and found you in that inn. Without you, I would have been captured by my uncle Harald and who knows what would have happened to me. Well, I guess it's pretty obvious what would have happened to me, I would have been killed."

"We have had some adventures, haven't we!" chortled Ganry, turning from the fire to look up at Myriam.

"You know that my grandmother will reward you richly for delivering me safely."

"I'm not here for the money. Not any more. I think my mercenary days are behind me."

"You could leave now if you want?" offered Myriam. "Zander can take me to Castle Locke. If you leave now you will be able to avoid Harald's troops and make your way to safety."

"I'm not leaving you now. If anyone is going to deliver you to your grandmother, it will be me."

"But you have risked so much for me," protested Myriam. "You have given up everything. You have even lost Bluebell. I owe my life to you."

"You have already given me something more valuable than all the gold in the kingdom. You have given me hope. You have given me a reason to live… a reason to fight… a reason to believe that the future might be worth sticking around for."

There was a small polite cough behind them.

"Oh, hello Ghaffar," said Myriam, turning to see the small monk standing behind them.

"I have come to say farewell," said Ghaffar.

"Must you go, Ghaffar? Won't you come with us?"

"My place is here in this forest," replied the monk, shaking his head.

"But won't the Lake Men be angry with you?" asked Ganry. "They will know that you have helped us, won't they?"

"I don't need to worry about the Lake Men," smiled Ghaffar. "They fear my knowledge, and they fear the water dragons that protect my temple. You will be safe now. Zander knows the way back to the Berghein Valley from here. Soon your journey will be over." Myriam embraced the monk warmly before he slipped away into the darkness. Remaining as much a mystery as ever.

"Somehow I don't feel as if my journey will end when we reach Castle Locke." Myriam stared off into the darkness that had swallowed the departing Ghaffar. "Somehow I feel that we're not even at the end of the beginning, if that makes sense."

"I think I know what you mean. However I guess the next move depends on what sort of reception we get when we reach your grandmother."

"How so?"

"Well, your grandmother has always been an ally of the Kingdom of Palara. She may not want to risk upsetting Harald by causing any sort of trouble. She may counsel that you simply accept that you have lost the crown, but be thankful that you have escaped with your life."

Myriam sat down on the floor next to Ganry. "I see your point, but Harald's treatment of my family is inexcusable. I have an obligation to the people of Palara to reclaim the throne, no matter what the cost is!"

"I thought you might say that. Why don't we ask Zander what his understanding of the situation is?"

Ganry and Myriam left the fire and walked across the clearing to where Zander was tending the horses.

"Princess, is everything okay?" asked Zander as they approached.

"Yes, I'm fine thank you, Zander. I was just wanting to ask you about my grandmother."

"The Duchess? Of course, what would you like to know?"

"Do you know what her intentions are?"

"I'm not sure that I understand you Princess, what do you mean by 'her intentions'?"

"I think what Myriam is interested in is whether you have any insight into what support the Duchess might be willing to offer Myriam in order to reclaim the throne of Palara," added Ganry.

"Oh, I see. To be honest, I'm not really sure. When she sent me on this mission to find you, her primary concern was your safety, and also that of your mother Alissia. At that stage I don't think she'd thought beyond bringing you to Castle Locke. I guess that doesn't really help you much."

"That's okay, thanks Zander," said Myriam. "Getting to Castle Locke is really all that I've been able to think of anyway. I'm not sure how I would go about raising an army, or launching some sort of attack on Harald."

"The Duchess has a lot of experience in how to wield power. She has ruled the Berghein Valley since the death of her father. She has had to defend her people countless times over the years. She won't be intimidated by any man, let alone by Duke Harald."

"I am looking forward to meeting the Duchess D'Anjou," grinned Ganry. "She sounds like quite a woman."

CHAPTER 48

"Explain yourself!" roared Clay, the chief of the Lake Men.

"I don't know what you're talking about, uncle," protested Linz.

"Do not take me for a fool!" Clay grabbed Linz roughly by the throat. "I should slice you into little pieces and feed you to the Polopons for your treachery! You have endangered us all! You have endangered the very existence of our people!"

"Brother! Please!" begged Linz's mother Lisl, grabbing hold of Clay's arm and trying to free her son from his grasp.

Clay slapped Lisl away with the back of his hand. "Silence! My men have told me that you took the prisoners from the fishing outpost. And now Myriam is missing. The girl that was to be your wife! Why would you dare to disobey me? To deceive me? To betray me?"

"I didn't want to marry Myriam. It made no sense. She's a princess." Linz was barely able to form the words due to his uncle's tight grip on his neck.

"What do you mean that you didn't want to marry her?" demanded the enraged Clay. "What you want or don't want is irrelevant here! If you are to lead this tribe then you need a wife."

"But you don't have a wife."

"Enough with your insolence!" Clay threw Linz to the floor of the wooden building that was their home. "Our very existence depends on us being invisible to the world beyond this forest, and you have thrown that away just because you don't want to take a wife. How dare you! How dare you!"

"Clay... please," sobbed Lisl. "He's just a boy, he didn't understand what he was doing. Please don't hurt him."

"Maybe it's time we stopped hiding, uncle? Maybe it's time that we took our place in this world?"

"Who are you to question our way of life?" glared Clay. "You may as well set a match to our homes or poison the lake on which we live. You know nothing of the struggles of our people, our fight to survive against the greed of the warrior Terrick."

"You have taught me everything I know. I am the man that you have made me to be."

"You are no man. You are a willful, impetuous boy. Get out of my sight." Lisl rushed to Linz to help him stand. "Get out of my sight! Now! Go!" raged Clay.

When they had returned to their own quarters, Lisl tended to the bumps and scrapes that Linz had suffered at the hands of his uncle.

"Why did you disobey him?" chided Lisl. "Why didn't you simply do as you were told and marry that girl?"

"I couldn't, mother. It was a silly idea to capture a princess, force her into marriage, and expect no consequences."

"You didn't find her attractive? I thought she was quite nice looking?"

"It wasn't that." Linz sighed, and shook his head sadly. He knew that he had disappointed his mother. He knew that he had angered his uncle. He knew that he hadn't been able to live up to their expectations, as ludicrous as they may have been.

"Hey, cheer up," soothed Lisl, mis-understanding the pain that her son was feeling. Lisl lent forward and kissed Linz on the forehead. "I'll speak with your uncle, when he has calmed down a little. It's best that you stay out of sight for a while. Why don't you hop into bed."

Leaving her son to rest, Lisl returned to her brother Clay who was still pacing and fuming.

"Did I hurt him?" asked Clay, concerned for the well-being of his nephew.

"He's okay, just a bit confused and upset. Have the scouts found anything?"

"It looks like that they've had assistance from the old monk who guards the river. They are beyond our reach now."

"Do you think we are in danger?"

"We are always in danger, but we have just lost the one advantage that we have always had - we are no longer hidden. We may need to leave this lake, head deeper into the forest, build a new home somewhere beyond the reach of the outside world."

"Perhaps there is another way?" suggested Lisl.

"What do you mean? What would you have me do?"

"Perhaps Linz has a point. Maybe it is time for us to stop hiding? If the girl Myriam took the throne of Palara, then she could grant us this lake as our own. It could be a way of protecting our future."

"But she is on the run from her uncle. She is unlikely to be of any use to us," dismissed Clay.

"I would like to send Linz to help her."

"Out of the question. The boy knows nothing of the outside world."

"He knows enough," insisted Lisl.

"What if he doesn't return? What if he never comes back? What then?"

"He is my son. He will come back. Let me take him to see the monk. I have a feeling that Linz could be the key to our future, not the end of our present."

"You talk in riddles, but I know better than to argue with you, sister. You were always far cleverer than I was."

"Linz reminds me a lot of you when you were younger," smiled Lisl.

Clay sighed. "That's what worries me."

CHAPTER 49

"What secrets do you hold within you?" Myriam hefted her dagger Harkan as she admired the sun's morning light glinting off the stones inlaid on its hilt. She held out her hand on which she wore the ring that also bore the same stonework. Next to each other they seemed to dazzle in the rays of the sun.

"Zander," asked Myriam, "can I have the dagger that my grandmother gave to you?"

"Of course Princess, here it is." Zander gave a small bow as he handed over the small blade that matched the ring and the dagger already held by Myriam.

Myriam carefully turned it over in her hands, studying the designs and engravings, comparing them, admiring them.

Barnaby approached and spoke softly. "Hendon has a ring just like yours. He wears it around his neck."

"Really?" said Myriam surprised. "Hendon?" She looked over her shoulder to where Hendon was talking with Artas. "Can I see your ring, please?"

"Of course." Hendon took off the chain around his neck which held the ring, holding it out towards Myriam as he approached her.

"Stay with me," she said, taking Hendon's ring in her hand. "Look at the stones... see how they're shining?"

"They're beautiful," acknowledged Hendon.

"In this light I can see more of the detail, more of the engravings on each piece." Myriam showed them to Hendon. "See how my ring and dagger have matching symbols? And look... the dagger that Zander was carrying, the one that was sent by my grandmother, it has the same symbols as your ring. Your ring and my grandmother's dagger are a pair. What do you think that means?"

Hendon studied the rings and daggers that Myriam held. "I don't know. It belonged to my mother. I don't know anything else about it."

"But where was your mother from?" pushed Myriam.

"I don't know... my father would never tell me anything about her."

"I can't believe that we found you that day in the forest just by accident. It's almost as if the stones were drawing us together, that we were meant to find each other."

"You know that you two look a bit alike," said Ganry bluntly, joining their conversation.

"Really?" asked Myriam. "Do you really think so?"

"I didn't see it at first, but the more time I spend with you, the more obvious it's becomes. There's something about the lines of your face that match each other. Maybe you're distant relations or something."

"And what do you think about the stones, Ganry? Have you ever seen anything like them before? Why do you think that they seem to shine brighter when they are close to each other?"

"They are pretty special, aren't they," admired Ganry, taking one of the daggers from Myriam's hand and turning it over carefully, as it caught the light of the morning sun. "They're not stones that I've ever seen before. They seem very old."

"Do you think that they could be magic?" asked Hendon.

"There's no such thing as magic, not that I've seen. There's no magic in stones, no magic in forests, no magic in animals, and no magic in water dragons that look like snakes."

"You seem to be pretty sure of that," laughed Myriam.

"Trust me," winked Ganry, "when you get to be as old as I am, you'll realize that if you want something in life you have to make it happen yourself. Wishing on a star, casting coins into a stream, kissing a rabbit, none of these things will make the slightest bit of difference. The only way that you can change the world around you or alter the course of your fate is if you do something about it."

"Maybe your problem, Ganry, is that you don't believe?" suggested Barnaby. "If you don't believe in magic then of course you won't understand it's power."

"Do you believe in magic, Barnaby?" asked Myriam.

"Of course," nodded the old man. "How else do you explain the fates bringing us together? How else do you explain our escape from the Lake Men? How else do you explain Zander being able to find us in the forest? There are clearly higher powers at work. We might not be able to see them or understand them, but that doesn't mean that there are not forces out there, guiding us, and protecting us."

"Fair enough, I guess we'll just have to agree to disagree. You believe in magic if you want, I'll continue to believe in the blade of my sword."

"Stop bickering you two!" laughed Myriam. "Hopefully grandmother will be able to shed some light on these mysteries when we get to Castle Locke. Meanwhile, I guess we'd better get moving. Lead on Zander! The Berghein Valley awaits!"

CHAPTER 50

Linz guided the small boat across the calm waters of the lake. "Are you sure that uncle is happy for us to do this?"

Lisl watched the sail as it flapped lazily in the wind. "Trust me, he understands. Take us into the monk's temple."

"But what about the water dragons that guard it?"

"We have nothing to fear. We are here as friends. The monk will welcome us. I can see that the lanterns are lit, that means he is at home."

Linz guided the boat alongside the wooden pier that jutted out into the lake, leaping from the boat in order to secure the moorings tightly.

"Madame Lisl," greeted Ghaffar warmly as he emerged from the temple. "It is a long time since I have seen you. Are you here on official business?"

"Hello Ghaffar. Yes, official business. I don't think you've met my son, Linz."

"A pleasure to meet you, sir," said Linz politely.

"Such good manners. You have trained him well, Madam Lisl."

"My brother would perhaps disagree with you," Lisl said, as they followed Ghaffar. "My son has proved to be rather rash and disobedient in recent times. I have come to you for help."

"How intriguing. It's unlike your brother to ask for help."

"To be fair it wasn't really his idea. He is still quite cross that you helped the foreigners escape from the lake. But in part, that is why we have come to you now. The Princess Myriam is traveling towards Castle Locke. I want you to take my son to join her there."

"You want me to take Linz away from the lake?" asked Ghaffar incredulously. "Do you expect some sort of union with Myriam?"

"Precisely the opposite," replied Lisl. "But it is time to end our isolation, and Myriam could be our one chance to maintain our independence. Linz can help her. He can help her claim the throne of Palara."

"With all due respect Madam Lisl, I think Myriam needs an army in order to claim the throne of Palara - I'm not sure that one young lake boy is going to make much of a difference."

"Please Ghaffar," insisted Lisl, "he has gifts… he has powers."

"For you Madam Lisl, anything. If it makes you happy I will take the boy to Castle Locke. But I won't be held responsible for any consequences that fall on your people as a result."

Lisl sailed by herself back to Halawa, the main settlement of the Lake Men. The morning breeze from the water ruffled her long brown hair. There was a chill in the air, but her fur cloak kept her warm. She felt as if a turning point of some kind had been reached. She felt strong. She knew in the heart that she had done the right thing.

As she entered the wooden building where she lived, Clay approached her. "He has gone?"

"Yes." Lisl calmly picked up some pieces of dried meat and dropped them gently into the pool of water that contained the polopon fish - their sharp teeth quickly tearing the meat apart as they churned the water excitedly.

"So what happens now?" asked Clay, perturbed by his sister's calmness.

"The monk will take Linz to Castle Locke in the Berghein Valley to meet Myriam. But nothing will change for us until she has been able to reclaim the throne."

"No sister, you're wrong," corrected Clay. "Everything has already changed for us. Everything. We have revealed our existence from those that our people have spent centuries hiding from. I have sent my heir out into their world. We will never be hidden again. There is every chance that the soldiers of Palara will be burning our villages down within a matter of weeks, if not days."

"Perhaps, but we have to have faith. Faith in Linz, but also faith that the gods will guide events in our favor."

"Did you make an offering at the monk's temple while you were there?"

"No, those are not my gods. I sacrificed a dove this morning, as the sun rose of the lake. Linz sat with me and we said the sacred words together."

"Good," nodded Clay. "I guess there is nothing more that we can do. Should we tell everyone what we have done?"

"There is no point alarming everyone, not until we hear from Linz. Once he can tell us how he has been received at Castle Locke, then we should tell them. Try not to worry Clay. Why don't you take me out in your boat, like we did when we were children?"

Clay's boat had always been his pride and joy. A small skiff, he had made it when he was thirteen. Their father had helped him to select the trees and prepare the wood. It had taken months of working on it every day to shape and form the hull of the craft. He had never felt prouder that when he had lifted the mast into place.

His father had made a speech when he had taken the boat out on to the water for the first time. He had been nervous, unsure if he had sealed it properly, anxious that the water would begin to seep through the wood that he had so carefully joined together. All of those fears were quickly forgotten as the wind filled the sail and the boat had begun to skim across the water. Every day when they were growing up, Clay had taken Lisl out in the boat. They had spent hours fishing together or just exploring the edges of the lake.

They had stopped the day that their father had been killed. Clay had had to assume his duties as chief of the tribe. Lisl got married, they had to grow up.

As the boat sailed across the water, Clay looked across at his sister. He felt like a child again.

CHAPTER 51

"We are nearly there, Princess," declared Zander. "Beyond that border post lies the Berghein Valley!" They had been traveling along the narrow forest trails, concealed by the trees as they made their way steadily west, west to safety.

As they looked down onto the guard post, still within the safety of the trees, they could see that the border was being heavily patrolled by Palaran soldiers.

Myriam was excited to be so close to the end of their long journey, but nervous also that there was still danger ahead. "How are we going to get past the guards?"

"We could create a distraction?" offered Ganry. "Create a skirmish to draw their attention, and that would enable you to push through the border."

"That's too dangerous, Ganry, you wouldn't stand a chance against numbers like this. I won't lose you now after you have brought me safely this far. There must be another way."

"Zander, is there not another way across the border?" asked Artas. "What about those cliffs? Is there a way that we could bypass this border post?"

"I imagine that they will have patrols all along the border, but maybe you have a point. We've always thought of the cliffs as being too unstable for anyone to use them as a crossing point, but these are desperate times. There are occasionally reports of bandits living in some of the small caves that have formed, and the paths are notoriously prone to collapse and avalanche, so it's just a question of which dangers we want to face."

"We'd have to leave the horses, though," said Ganry. "They're not going to be able to take those cliff paths."

"That is true," agreed Zander, "but there is a farming settlement near the base of the cliffs, and we would be able to commandeer some horses there for the final leg of our journey to Castle Locke."

"What do you think, Princess?" asked Ganry. Myriam scanned the blue skies that stretched as far as the eye could see. A lone eagle circled high overhead, occasionally calling out a lonesome cry as it searched for prey in the grassland below.

"Let's tackle the cliffs," decided Myriam. "Lead on Zander! If any bandits get in our way they had better watch out. The stones in my dagger are glowing brightly and I am in no mood for being messed around!"

"She used to be such a sweet girl," grumbled Ganry to Artas.

"I heard that Ganry!" shouted Myriam. "I'm going to make you walk in front to test whether the cliff trails will take our weight!"

Ganry took charge of removing the saddles from the horses and setting them loose. Zander and his men re-packed their rucksacks, leaving behind anything that was not essential, trying to make their load as light as possible for the climb.

"Are you ready for this, Barnaby?" asked Hendon, concerned that the strenuous ascent might be too much for the old man.

"Don't you worry about me," winked Barnaby. "I might be old but I can keep up with you."

"We have a short distance from the edge of the tree-line through into that first rocky outcrop. We will be exposed, and it is possible that we will be spotted by their scouts, so we need to make sure that we move as fast as possible," explained Zander. "I will lead the way. Karam will take the back. Aban, Yasir, and Najid will protect the flanks. If we are detected at all you have to keep moving and we will engage with the enemy. Ganry, if you stay with Myriam then you can keep her safe and keep moving forward with her if there is any trouble. If all goes well then we'll stop and get our bearings once we reach the protection of the rocks. If there is trouble then just keep moving and push as far up into the cliffs as possible. Any questions?"

Ganry approved. "Sounds like a good plan."

"Right, on my lead, leave a count of two between each other so that we are not tripping over ourselves. Ready... Now!" Zander suddenly leapt forward and was sprinting across the open ground, keeping low to try and avoid attracting any attention from the Palaran scouts. After a count of two, Artas leapt forward and quickly followed in Zander's footsteps. Next went Aban, Yasir, and Najid to create a protective flank. Then it was Ganry and Myriam, running together. Barnaby was next, then Hendon, and finally Karam brought up the rear.

When they had been scoping out the route to be taken from the safety of the trees, it hadn't seemed so far, but now - with his heart pumping and his legs moving as fast as possible, Ganry could feel his body straining. Beside him Myriam was moving smoothly, composed and calm as they quickly covered the open ground. The rocky outcrop was in sight now, they could see that Zander had nearly made it to safety.

"Quickly! Hurry now!" hissed Zander. An arrow suddenly thwacked into the ground close to Ganry's foot.

"Damn it... they've seen us! We have to move faster!" urged Ganry, trying to see which direction the archers might be shooting from so that he could try and protect Myriam. The arrows began to fall increasingly thickly. Ganry could see that Artas had made it to the safety of the rocks and had quickly notched an arrow into his bow, trying to see where they were shooting from, trying to see whether he could take them out and protect the others. Artas loosed several arrows but still the attack came. Eventually Ganry and Myriam made it to the safety of the rocks.

"Keep moving!" urged Zander. "Don't wait for us, push higher! Artas can stay with me to try and hold them off."

"I can't leave without making sure that everyone is safe!" protested Myriam.

"You have to go now, Princess!" insisted Zander. "Ganry, keep moving, find a defensible position and wait for us if you can. We won't be far behind. Go!" Garny grabbed Myriam by the arm and almost dragged her onto the trail that was heading higher into the cliffs. Behind them they could hear the arrows clattering onto the rocks that were sheltering Zander and Artas.

"This path is going to get steep pretty quickly." Ganry cautiously tested the loose rocks that were already feeling like they were shifting beneath his feet.

Myriam looked back over her shoulder to see whether she could see any sign of her companions. "Can we not wait for them here?"

"Not yet, we're too exposed, we need to keep moving. Come on, a bit further. We can rest in a moment."

Back down at the rocky outcrop, Zander was becoming increasingly worried as the arrows continued to rain down on them. Hendon and Yasir had only just made it to safety, but Barnaby had been wounded in the leg, and Aban and Najid were trying to carry him the rest of the way. Zander knew that even if they got to the rock that Barnaby wouldn't be able to cope with the steep narrow cliff paths that lay ahead of them.

"Karam! Karam! Quickly! Get to safety!" shouted Zander. As Karam dived beneath the cover of the rocks, Zander looked out and saw the arrows embedding themselves deep into the bodies of his men. Aban fell first, then Najid. Unprotected, Barnaby also lost his life to the cold stabbing pain of an arrow in the chest.

"No! Barnaby!" wailed Hendon, watching on as his friend fell.

"We need to move now!" ordered Zander. "They will be coming for us!"

"We can't leave him there!" sobbed Hendon, wrestling against Artas who was trying to restrain him from dashing back out towards Barnaby's dead body.

"We have to. We have no choice. If we don't go now we will all be killed. Yasir, quickly, lead the way!"

Yasir began to bound up the steep slope of the cliff, picking his way between the loose rocks. Artas, dragging the bereft Hendon behind him, followed after, with Karam and Zander bringing up the rear.

Up ahead, Ganry had found a small ledge where the cliff path narrowed. Confident that he could overpower anyone who tried to approach, they had decided to wait for the others. Ganry had his trusty sword WindStorm, guarding the approach, while Myriam stood behind him with her blade Harkan drawn - the stones in its hilt shining brightly.

"Ganry! We are approaching!" shouted Yasir, seeing the light reflect off Ganry's drawn blade.

"They made it!" gasped Myriam, immediately sheathing her dagger. They gathered on the small ledge, quickly trying to catch their breath after the strenuous sprint to safety and the steep ascent that they had had to make. It took a moment for Myriam and Ganry to realize that their numbers were fewer.

"Aban? Najid? Wait... where's Barnaby? No... No... Please no." Myriam could see from Hendon's ashen face that Barnaby hadn't made it to safety. She wrapped her arms around him and tried to console him.

"We have to keep moving." Zander's breathing had steadied, he was ready to continue. "Their arrows won't be much of a threat now but they will come after us on foot. They won't be far behind."

Ganry shielded his eyes from the sun, and tried to see if he could spot any pursuers. "Should we try and block this path in some way?"

"We could create a landslide without too much difficulty. But I think it's better if we just focus on moving as quickly as we can. We need to head up towards that peak and then work our way down to the valley floor. Yasir, lead the way. Let's move."

Treading carefully but as quickly as they dared, the companions moved in single file along the narrow cliff path, frequently dislodging loose stones beneath their feet that tumbled far down beneath them.

"I see them!" pointed Artas, looking back at the path below them. "There looks to be about ten of them!"

"What's your aim like with that bow?" asked Zander.

"I've never seen better," said Ganry, with a nod towards Artas.

"See how many you can take out, Artas. It will slow them down at the very least."

Artas positioned himself on a small outcrop and notched an arrow into his bow, patiently taking aim and waiting for a clear shot at the soldiers that were working their way up the cliff towards them.

Zander and the others continued to push forward, continued to push up. The top of the cliff was in sight and they were beginning to feel that they had a chance at reaching their goal, of reaching safety.

Myriam looked back at the sound of falling rocks and could see one of the soldiers of Palara falling lifelessly down the side of the cliff, snared by one of Artas' arrows. "Please, can we wait for him?"

"He wouldn't want us to. He'll catch us up. He'll be moving faster than us anyway. Don't worry, I've got a lot of faith in Artas," replied Ganry.

"We're nearly at the top," urged Zander. "We'll stop there and wait for Artas."

At the top of the cliff Myriam gasped in delight as the Berghein Valley was revealed below.

"I can't believe we've made it!" exclaimed Myriam.

"We haven't made it yet," cautioned Ganry. "But at least here comes Artas! How many left, Artas?"

"There's at least five still on the path." Artas panted from his sprint.

"Why don't we wait here and finish them off?" Ganry was eager for WindStorm to sing.

Zander thought about it for a beat. "Yes, I think you're right. We can't risk drawing them down into the village. If there are only five then we will be able to overpower them, given we have the advantage. Quickly, let's conceal ourselves and wait for them."

Myriam could feel her heart pounding as she tried to control her breathing, while they lay in wait for the pursuing soldiers. It seemed like they had been hidden for an eternity, and she began to wonder whether they had perhaps given up the chase and turned back. Just as she was about to say something, she heard the scuffling of feet along the stony path, the clinking of weapons being carried. Myriam clutched Harkan, her knife, tightly, drawing strength from the glowing stones. As the soldiers from Palara rounded the bend at the top of the cliff, there was a deafening roar as Ganry leapt from his hiding place, wielding his sword and shouting.

There was a tremendous clash of metal, screams of dying men, and then an eerie silence. When Myriam emerged from behind the rock where she had been hiding, she saw Ganry standing proudly with the soldiers at his feet. The mercenary had done his work.

CHAPTER 52

"What sort of reception do you think we will get at Castle Locke?" asked Yazid, riding beside Qutaybah as they made the journey from Villa Salamah in Vandemland, and across the border into the Berghein Valley.

"She will be pleased to see us, I imagine."

"Have you met the Duchess before?"

"No, never," replied Qutaybah, "but I have heard plenty of stories about her."

"Does she really have powers?"

Qutaybah raised an eyebrow. "What sort of powers do you speak of?"

"You call her a witch… and I have heard others speak of her as being some kind of mystic."

Arexos was riding behind Qutaybah and Yazid. He remained silent but he was intensely interested in their conversation - any talk of magic intrigued him.

"You shouldn't believe fairytales!" laughed Qutaybah. "There is no such thing as magical powers. The Duchess is just a clever woman who knows how to rule.

Her power is her mind, and her ability to outwit the foolish men that attempt to control her. Some men see that as witchcraft."

The border crossing between Vandemland and the Berghein Valley was controlled by small guard-posts on either side. The party of one hundred soldiers on horseback from Vandemland caused some concern at the Berghein Valley guard-post, but Qutaybah had a letter of invitation from the Duchess which quickly secured their safe passage.

It was Captain Versance, the Duchess's captain of the guard, who rode out to greet the approaching party from Vandemland, escorting them to the barracks that had been assigned to them and arranging for the stable-hands to tend to their horses.

"The Duchess is ready to receive you at your earliest convenience, Master Qutaybah."

"Excellent, shall I bring my deputy with me?"

"I think it would be perhaps best if you met with the Duchess alone."

"Of course, captain, please, lead the way. I do not want to keep the Duchess waiting."

The Duchess received Qutaybah in her study. The light was shining brightly through the windows, illuminating the room and catching the silver thread that was embroidered on the blue dress that she wore. The Duchess stood as Qutaybah was shown into the room.

"Master Qutaybah, welcome," smiled the Duchess, inclining her head slightly. "I am grateful that you have answered my call for help."

"Your Excellence, it is indeed an honor to meet you," bowed Qutaybah respectfully.

"Well, to coin an old phrase, we live in interesting times. Our friends become our enemies and our neighbors become our allies. I'm sure your networks of intelligence gatherers and informers will have kept you abreast of our troubles, but I imagine that you are not exactly sure why I have reached out to you."

"You are indeed correct, Your Excellence. The turmoil within the Kingdom of Palara is known to me, as are your personal tragedies. I am sorry for the loss of your daughter," proffered Qutaybah.

"Thank you for your kindness," acknowledged the Duchess. "The good news is that I believe that my granddaughter is safe. My granddaughter is the rightful heir to the throne of Palara. It is her claim to the throne that is the reason that I have sought your assistance."

"You intend to attack Duke Harald? You will march on the Kingdom of Palara?"

"Yes. Yes…and no."

"I'm not quite sure I follow you?"

"As I'm sure you're aware, Duke Harald has amassed a sizeable army, plus he has built an impressive naval fleet. All of this was designed to launch a full-scale assault against the Caliphate of Vandemland, but it seems that he intends first to cut his teeth against the people of the Berghein Valley," explained the Duchess. "Of course, my small army will be no match for him. His forces will crush us within a matter of days, if not hours."

"So you will not march against him?" asked Qutaybah, beginning to feel confused.

"I will distract him. I will draw his eye towards the Berghein Valley, towards Castle Locke... and while I draw his eye, I want you to kill him."

CHAPTER 53

The druids' temple lay in ruins. Duke Harald's men had been merciless. Zaim, the arms-bearer, had done as instructed and lain waste to the druids and their living quarters, setting fire to the wooden buildings and destroying the stone monuments.

After killing the druids, Zaim's men had loaded the barrels of fire-powder onto the druids' wagons to transport them back to Castle Villeroy. The bodies of the men that had been slain lay scattered throughout the temple grounds, across the garden beds where they had grown vegetables, across the alters at which they had prayed, slain while trying to protect the ancient artifacts and relics that were used in their ceremonies and prayers.

As the wagons rolled through the surrounding farmlands, the villagers looked on in stunned silence, unable to comprehend the changing world in which they lived. A world in which the sacred and revered druids could be so brutally cast aside, the gods and temples that had been worshiped so easily desecrated.

"Excellent! This is exactly what we need," exclaimed Duke Harald as he inspected the barrels that had been forcibly confiscated from the druids.

"Have you used the druid's fire-powder before, sir?" asked Zaim.

"No, we will need to test it. We need to trial it against something that is of similar thickness to the walls of Castle Locke. We're going to need to be able to blast that old witch out of her nest."

"There is the old fort that protects the bridge at Athacar. Of course, it is quite useful as a strategic defense, but it's the only thing that I can think of with thick walls apart from the castle here."

"Well we're not blowing up Castle Villeroy! We either blow up the fort or we try and tackle Castle Locke without any clue as to how much fire-powder we would need to get the job done. Let's assemble a small advance party and march towards Athacar with the barrels of fire-powder. The rest of the army can be mobilized to join us when we are ready to launch our attack against Castle Locke."

It was a party of several hundred soldiers that were tasked with transporting the wagons loaded with fire-powder along the road westwards towards the town of Athacar. Harald surveyed the old stone fort - a remnant of the days of Chief Terrick who had united the tribes.

"We're going to need a point in the wall where we can dig down towards the foundations." Harald tried to visualize how they would most effectively launch an attack against Castle Locke. "So, we're going to need to have some sort of protection overhead to enable us to dig. We create a hole at the bottom of the wall, pack it tightly with the barrels of fire-powder, and then light it up. The force of the explosion should be enough to create a breach in the wall that we can then break through and crush their defenses."

"But how many barrels of fire-powder do we need to use in order to create a big enough explosion?" asked Zaim.

"That's what we're here to test out. Let's start with ten and see what sort of mess that makes."

Zaim took charge of overseeing the digging operations, while also tasking his men to build several different types of contraptions that could provide some sort of overhead protection. The main concern would be arrows being fired down from the walls, but fire and hot oil were also commonly used by defenders trying to repel a siege. Eventually Zaim reported back to Harald that they had created a hole at the foundations of the wall of the old fort and packed it with ten barrels of the druids' fire-powder.

"We can light it with a flaming arrow. That will give us enough time to get our men clear of the explosion."

"Excellent!" Harald rubbed his palms together in anticipation. "Well, let's see what happens!"

As the dust slowly cleared, Harald was beaming with delight as he surveyed the ruined wall of the old fort.

"Castle Locke doesn't stand a chance!" laughed the Duke, surveying the destruction that lay at his feet.

CHAPTER 54

"Myriam my child, you have made it!" The Duchess was waiting at the gates of the castle, immediately hugging Myriam as soon as she had been helped down from the horse that had carried her across the Berghein Valley.

"Grandmother!" gasped Myriam. It felt slightly surreal to be in the arms of this woman, a woman she had met a long time ago when the world had seemed to be a different place, a safer place. "I have so much to ask you, so many questions!"

"Shhh.... there will be time for questions. But first we must care for you. You need food, you need to bathe, you need to rest. Come, go with the maids and I will come and sit with you in a moment." The Duchess turned to the rest of the waiting party. Ganry could sense a steeliness in her. She was clearly a woman that was in control, a determined woman who knew what needed to be done.

"Zander, you have impressed me yet again. Well done."

"Thank you, Your Excellence," bowed Zander deeply.

"Introduce me to the rest of the party."

"These are my men, Yasir and Karam; this is Ganry and Artas who have traveled with Myriam since her escape from Castle Villeroy, and this is Hendon, who I believe they met in the Cefinon Forest."

Ganry could feel the Duchess's eyes fall on each of them, assessing them somehow, processing the information that Zander was providing.

"You each have my utmost gratitude. I can only imagine the hardships that you have suffered together on your escape from Palara. Your commitment to protecting my granddaughter is proof not only of your loyalty, but also your immense courage and bravery. I am sure that we have much to talk about, but I can see that you are all exhausted. Please, follow the household staff and they will help you with food, bathing, and fresh clothes." The companions gratefully began to move towards the castle doors where food and rest waited for them. "Hendon," said the Duchess suddenly. "A moment please, I would like just a quick word with you before you join the others."

There was a quiet knock on the door of the sleeping quarters to which Myriam has been assigned.

"May I come in?" asked the Duchess politely.

"Of course Grandmother! Of course," beamed Myriam. "I can't quite believe that I am really here. It all feels a bit unreal at the moment, if that makes sense?"

"It makes perfect sense my dear, you've had quite an ordeal."

"Grandmother, I know that you said that there would be time for questions later. But, please, can I ask… my mother and father… they're dead aren't they?"

The Duchess took Myriam in her arms and held her close. "Yes dear… I'm afraid so. I felt it too as I'm sure you did. And Hendon felt it as well…"

"Hendon," murmured Myriam. "Yes, Hendon! Who is Hendon? Why do I feel such a connection to him? How does he have a ring that matches the dagger that you sent with Zander?"

"Shhh now," soothed the Duchess, "don't get yourself all worked up. All will be revealed in good time. But you need to know that Hendon is a part of me, just as much as you are."

"But… how can that be?" asked Myriam, looking up at her grandmother.

"Shhh now… all in good time."

After bathing and eating, Artas had gone for a walk out along the walls of the castle, finally feeling as if he was able to breath, finally, for a moment at least, not looking over his shoulder, waiting for danger at every turn. Artas was staring out across the plains of the Berghein Valley when he heard a voice behind him.

"Hello," said the voice. Artas turned to see who it was that was talking to him. The face looked familiar, but it was strangely out of context. Artas tried to piece together the puzzle that was before him. A face he knew but somehow didn't recognize. Finally it dawned on him.

"Linz? Linz? Is it really you? What are you doing here?" gasped Artas.

"They said that you had gone for a walk, I came to find you."

"No, I mean, we left you back at the lake... you rescued us... how are you here now at Castle Locke? I thought it was forbidden for you to leave?"

"It's all been a bit of a blur, to be honest." Linz shook his head quickly, as though trying to juggle his memories into some sort of order. "After you left, nothing seemed the same. My mother persuaded my father to let me come and try and help Myriam regain the throne of Palara."

"But how did you manage to make the journey to Castle Locke? We've only just survived. We lost several of our companions to the arrows of the soldiers," said Artas sadly.

"I'm sorry for your loss. The monk Ghaffar traveled with me. He seems to be able to travel without attracting too much attention to himself."

"Ghaffar that old fox!" laughed Artas. "I should have known that we hadn't seen the last of him. Well... I must say that I am glad to see you again. I feared that we would never have the chance to spend any time together."

"I'm glad too," smiled Linz. "I'm glad too."

"You asked to see me, Your Excellency?" asked Ganry, cautiously entering the Duchess's study.

"Ganry, please come in," instructed the Duchess. "No one seems to know very much about you, but my granddaughter speaks very highly of you and that is all

I need to know. I am under no illusion that she would not have been able to survive without your care and attention."

"It has been my pleasure, Your Excellence."

"I understand that Leonidavus, Myriam's tutor, paid you a small fee to transport her here. I am happy to double that. I will have the gold prepared so that you can collect your reward and be released from your obligations."

"Your Excellence? I'm sorry, I'm not sure I understand."

"It's not enough? You demand more gold?" asked the Duchess.

"No, no, not at all. It's just that... I don't really want to be released from my obligations."

"You are a mercenary, are you not? You have completed your mission and you should be rewarded for that," pointed out the Duchess.

"I think perhaps that my mercenary days might be over," said Ganry slowly. "No amount of gold in the world can make me walk away from Myriam now. I need to see this through. I need to help her reclaim the throne of Palara. I need to help her free her people."

"You haven't developed some sort of ridiculous romantic attachment to her have you?" snapped the Duchess.

"No, not at all, quite the contrary," explained Ganry quickly. "I think of her as a daughter. She reminds me of the daughter that I lost long ago."

"I see," nodded the Duchess approvingly. "I can see that she was right to trust you. Good."

"Good?" asked Ganry, not sure exactly what the Duchess meant by this.

"Yes. Good," affirmed the Duchess. "We have difficult days ahead. My granddaughter will need all of her friends and allies beside her. I want you to be her personal bodyguard. I want you to promise me that you will protect her."

"Of course, Your Excellence, I promise to protect her with my life."

The Duchess walked to a window and stared out across the valley below. "He's coming for her," she said quietly, staring into the distance.

"Duke Harald?" asked Ganry, unsure if the statement had been directed towards him, unsure if he was required to give a response.

"Yes... he's coming for her," repeated the Duchess. "He will not rest until he has killed her. He will march his armies against us and will crush everything that stands in his way."

"Should I take her away? Take her somewhere safe?"

"No. There isn't anywhere. Nowhere is safe. She must remain here. She is the bait that will draw that snake in."

"You're using Myriam as bait?" Ganry was not really sure that he had heard the Duchess correctly. "Isn't that a fairly risky strategy?"

"Ganry," said the Duchess, turning towards him with a smile, "in this game the only way to win is to risk it all."

CHAPTER 55

The bells in the towers of Castle Locke sounded the call to arms. Captain Versance had assembled the army of the Berghein Valley. The farmers, the tradesmen - they had trained them as much as possible, they had equipped them with as many weapons as possible, but as Captain Versance surveyed the faces of his men he knew that it wouldn't be enough.

"We are no match for what marches towards our borders," observed Zander Moncrieff, seeing the concern on the captain's face.

"This is madness," said the captain.

"I don't think it would be wise to accuse the Duchess of madness," chuckled Zander lightly. "At least, not to her face. These walls are built to withstand a siege. We just need to hold them as long as possible."

"Is that the plan then?" asked Captain Versance. "Try and sit out a siege?"

"I think that is part of the plan, but I have to confess that the Duchess hasn't taken me fully into her confidence as to how she intends to defeat Duke Harald. I think it's interesting though that the battalion from Vandemland have moved out."

"They rode off towards Vandemland," replied the captain. "I assumed that they were heading home, not prepared to sign up to a lost cause?"

"Oh, I don't think that's the case at all. I don't think we've seen the last of our friends from Vandemland. We live in interesting times old friend... we live in interesting times."

The Duchess sat in her study. On one side of her sat Myriam, on the other side Hendon. The three of them wore the rings of Berghein, the stones glowing brightly, almost shining as they reflected and amplified the suns rays. In front of each of them sat their matching dagger. Myriam reached out and caressed the bade of Harkan - the name of the blade, the name that had been told to her by Leonidavus her tutor when he had given it to her.

"Ready?" asked the Duchess quietly, looking at first to Myriam and then Hendon. They both nodded solemnly. The Duchess demonstrated what had to be done. They each took hold of the dagger in front of them and ran the sharp blade across the palm of their left hand. As the blood began to flow from their self-inflicted wounds, the Duchess showed them how to hold their hands over the silver bowl that sat in the middle of the small wooden table. They watched silently as their blood began to drip steadily down into the bowl, collecting and combining as it formed a small crimson pool.

"Close your eyes now," instructed the Duchess, "and visualize our future. Visualize a future where the Berghein Valley is safe once more. Visualize a future where Duke Harald has been defeated. Visualize a future where Myriam has been crowned as the rightful ruler of the Kingdom of Palara. Now we must visualize the sun setting and rising three times... dusk to dawn... dusk to dawn... dusk to dawn... together we create the future... There... you can open your eyes now."

"Does it work, Grandmother?" asked Myriam in hushed tones, in awe of the command and control that the Duchess displayed.

Hendon was wide-eyed. "Is it magic?"

"Now Hendon... there's no such thing as magic," the Duchess' eyes twinkled, "but we know that we are stronger together, that when we put our hearts and minds together there is nothing that can stand in our way. We know that our blood comes from an ancient line of kings, and that when we choose to spill our blood for something that we believe in, something we are passionate about, then the earth will tremble before us, and we will reach for the stars."

Hendon nodded his understanding. "The bells are ringing. What does that mean?"

"It means that a storm is coming. A storm that will change the world for all of us. But we have to have faith that the future that we have visualized is the future that will come to pass."

There was a gentle knock on the door.

"Yes?" said the Duchess. It was Ganry.

"I'm sorry to interrupt, Your Excellence."Ganry bowed respectfully. "I think it's time that Myriam and Hendon came with me."

"You're quite right, Ganry."

"But we're not leaving you, are we grandmother?" protested Myriam.

"No child, you're not leaving me. Remember, we are stronger together. But I have asked Ganry to keep you both safe. No matter what happens you must listen to him and trust that he is looking after your best interests. Any day now our castle will be under siege, there is a strong chance that our walls will be breached. The castle keep is the most secure part. It will be the last to fall. If all else fails, beneath the keep is a tunnel that will take you away from the castle and then it will be up to Ganry to keep you safe."

"Grandmother, I'm scared," whispered Myriam, hugging the Duchess tightly.

"Turn that fear into determination. We must not be bowed, we must not crumble, the old world may fall but the House of Locke must rise from the ashes like a phoenix from the flames. From dusk until dawn my children!"

As Ganry led Myriam and Hendon out of the Duchess's study and down towards the keep that would be their stronghold for the duration of the impending battle, the Duchess looked from the window of her study out across the plains of the Berghein Valley.

"A storm is coming," she said quietly to herself. "A storm is coming."

ABOUT THE AUTHOR

Jon Kiln writes heroic fantasy. His major influences include David Gemmell and Conn Iggulden.

Sign up to his mailing list or contact him at
www.JonKiln.com

Printed in Great Britain
by Amazon.co.uk, Ltd.,
Marston Gate.